ONE NIGHT

ALEATHA ROMIG

Edited by LISA AURELLO

Photography by WANDER AGUIAR

Cover Art by LETITIA HASSER RBA DESIGNS ROMANTIC BOOK AFFAIRS

Formatted by ROMIG WORKS LLC

Romig Works LLC

ALEATHA ROMIG

New York Times, Wall Street Journal, and USA Today bestselling
author of the Infidelity and Consequences series and PLUS ONE

COPYRIGHT AND LICENSE INFORMATION

either are the product of the author's imagination or are used fictitiously, and any resemblance to any actual persons, living or dead, events, or locales is entirely coincidental.

This book is available in print from most online retailers

2017 Edition License

AUTHOR'S Note

Over a year ago my friend Georgia Cates and I decided to start an adventure: writing stories that were outside of our brand. Our endeavor was successful on many counts. It opened a world of possibilities and let us shake off the chains of expectation. Though we each wrote different titles, we ventured into that new world under one name.

While that pen name no longer exists, it helped us to expand our horizons and try new things.

The story you're about to read started as a short and sexy, predictable novella written by me as Jade Sinner and entitled MALCOLM: The Meeting. My reviews were good and I learned that while writing dark twists and turns, I could also be funny and light.

If any part of this story seems familiar, it could be because you read the 17K-word short novella. That was just the beginning.

ONE NIGHT is more! It is now a full-length, contemporary romantic-comedy novel.

I hope it makes you swoon, laugh, maybe shed a tear or two, and finish the last page with a smile.

I know that I did all of that while writing.

Thank you for allowing me to shed the other name and embrace this side of Aleatha. Thank you for giving Leatha, the lighter side of Aleatha, a chance!

I hope you enjoy ONE NIGHT!

ONE *night*

A sweet, fun, and sexy stand-alone romance from New York Times bestselling author Aleatha Romig.

One night to remember

Is that too much to desire?

One night for fun, passion, and a chance to remember what it's like to be a woman.

I'm not looking for love.

There's a man in my life who loves me with all his heart. He has beautiful blue eyes, is three feet tall, and calls me mommy.

He's my whole world and I'm his. Fate stole away his daddy far too soon.

What would happen if I allowed fate another chance, just for one night?

One night to help a friend

Why did I agree to this?

Blind dates are disasters. If I weren't helping the friend of a friend, I wouldn't go.

I'm not looking for romance, love, or even a one-night stand.

After all, the man my friend knew is gone. I'm no longer the hockey star known for his "pep" on the ice and in the sack. I have a new life and a new career—a new passion. I'm not looking for more.

When the blind date is a bust, could fate change everything?

One night doesn't end with a kiss—it begins with one.

Be ready to laugh, cry, and fall head over heels in love as you let Leatha, the lighter side of Aleatha, take you away with this new, sweet, and sexy stand-alone romance, ONE NIGHT, the perfect reading to keep you warm...hot... steamy...on a cool night.

ONE Night

CHAPTER

Amanda

The hum of the office around me disappears as I notice the small clock at the bottom of my computer screen. How did I miss lunch again?

I shake my head and reach for my emergency stash, hidden at the back of my desk drawer. A protein bar isn't exactly the lunch of champions—or the breakfast—but more often than not it's what I end up eating. Maybe I should think of a better stash. Like those little tiny wine bottles. If I drank a white, I could pretend that it's water.

Instead, I unscrew the cap from my real water bottle and take another bite of my protein bar.

"Oh my God," Sally says as she slips into my cubicle. "Tell me that's a midafternoon snack and not your lunch."

"I would but..." The words come out scratchy from the dry oatmeal and peanut butter that's currently working more as a glue to keep my lips stuck to my teeth. I wiggle my lips as I try to swallow.

"Seriously, I texted you about lunch."

I down a gulp of water and pry my lips from my teeth. "I know. I saw it. But Cruella de Vil has been on the warpath today."

We both turn as an interoffice communication pings from my computer and my manager's name appears on the screen.

"See," I say.

Sally laughs. "Have you thought about Friday night?"

"Are you serious? I didn't have a chance to remember lunch; Friday night is too much for me to think about right now."

She settles her behind against the edge of my desk. Crossing her arms over her chest, she lowers her voice. "I promise you'll like him."

"I'm not you."

"That's good. I'm seeing someone. I can't go on a blind date."

My nose scrunches. "Why do they call them that? Even the idea makes my skin crawl."

Sally is my best-est and longest friend. We've been like two peas in a pod since we were young, since the time we both discovered that boys weren't just smelly, cocky pests, but actually had appeal. A lot of appeal. We've seen each other through life's ups and downs. It's true that her life has had a few more ups, but no matter what, we've been there for one another.

"Oh, sweetie," Sally goes on, "Brian's friend Pep will NOT make your skin crawl. No...those goose bumps will all be from the heat."

"Sally, seriously, I'm not ready."

"You are. You need to be. It's just a date."

My bottom lip disappears between my teeth for only a moment. It's been a long time since I've thrown caution to the wind and let myself go. One night of abandoned, reckless fun. How difficult would that be to do? Would I even remember how?

"See," she says with a knowing grin. "You're thinking about it. You're actually considering it."

My computer pings and I turn back to the screen. It's another message from my manager, no doubt reminding me about something she's reminded me about fifty times, or maybe it's a new trivial task that she's come up with for me. God knows messaging me to email someone takes her more time than if she'd actually write the damn email herself.

Shaking my head, I look back at my friend's big hazel eyes.

She bats her eyelashes and opens them wide as she tries one more time. "Okay, I wasn't going to tell you this, but even though he's new in town, gorgeous, funny, and sexy as hell, we're worried."

"You're worried?"

"Well, Brian more than I. I've only met him once and he seems really nice. It's just that Brian's concerned that there could be something wrong with him."

"Like what?" I ask.

Her head tilts to the side. "Come on, Amanda. You'd be helping the poor guy out, and I know how partial you are to helping the less fortunate."

"I leave food out for the puppies and kitties. I volunteer at the homeless shelter at least once a month. I'm not in the habit of helping twenty- to thirty-something-year-old men."

"Hey, those men need a little help sometimes too. I never thought you would discriminate. I mean, what if he was at the shelter?"

"He's homeless?"

"No. But doesn't everyone deserve a little help now and then?"

I take a deep breath, my attention torn between Sally and the persistent pinging of my computer messages. "All right, spill. What's wrong with him? Is he color-blind? Dyslexic? Does he have one testicle that's smaller than the other?"

I cover my grin as my eyes open wide. Only with Sally would I say such a thing.

She leans closer. "Well, I'm not sure about his testicle. You see, Brian and I made this bet. Brian thinks that his old friend may have an issue with getting it up...too many PED's when he played for the Lightning." She shrugs. "That's what Brian thinks. Me, I think that he has a playboy rock-hard body with a soft heart and just hasn't found the right lady."

"Wait a minute. Are you saying you want me, hardly playboy-girlfriend material, to settle your bet?"

"No," Sally insists. "I want you to be that right lady. And," she adds with a grin, "Brian wants to know if he can get it up."

I shake my head. "That sounds like too much work. Besides,

I'm taken. I have the handsomest man in my life. As a matter of fact, he slept in my bed last night."

"Jase doesn't count."

"What do you mean?" I mock shock. "He most certainly can count. He has since he was three. He also knows his ABC's. Actually, he's a genius and you, Aunt Sally, should know that. He can even write his name, first and last."

"Honey, you're a great mom. But it's not fair to you—or to Jase —to live like a monk. It's time to see what the world has to offer."

Again, my computer pings.

"Ugh. I don't think monks have a million messages backing up. Besides, don't they take a vow of silence or something?"

"Then a nun," Sally replies. "That's it. You're right. You make a better nun. Celibate and wine drinking."

"Hey!" I reach up to my long brown hair, currently pulled to the side in a low ponytail resting on my shoulder. "I could never wear a habit. Can you imagine how flat that would make my hair?"

Sally laughs. "Speaking of habits. Try giving up that celibate thing and I know a habit you'll enjoy again."

I purse my lips. "I don't know. My parents are always willing to watch Jase, but he goes to bed at eight-thirty. I'm sure Mr. Sexy-ex-hockey-player slash rock-hard-playboy isn't interested in a date that turns into a pumpkin at eight o'clock, even if he does have erection issues."

"I bet if you ask nicely, your parents will keep Jase overnight. As a matter of fact, I know they will."

"You know?" I ask suspiciously as my stomach twists.

I'm not ready for this. I should be. Jason just turned five years old and it's been nearly five years since I last saw his father. The memories incite the same emotions they always do. I see his blue eyes, the same ones I see daily in our son. I remember his parting words, telling me he'd return safe and sound. I remember the touch of his lips on mine just before he pulled away from me and headed toward his unit. And then I remember the terrible knock on the door. I knew what had happened before I opened it. No military wife wants to see a man in uniform at her front door who isn't her husband.

The following few weeks are still a blur. I can't remember how I functioned, if I ate, or if I even took care of Jase. He was so young. I tried. Thank God for my parents.

Somehow we survived. Somehow time has moved on.

In a few days, Jason will begin kindergarten as a relatively well-adjusted little man. I couldn't be prouder of him, and I know Jackson would be too. That's why I let Jase consume my life: he deserves more than what I can give. He deserves two parents. Thanks to a roadside IED, it's up to me to be both.

Yet there are times that I wonder what it would be like to be a twenty-five-year-old woman, instead of the responsible mother, if only for one night.

Ping!

"Shit, Sally, I need to get on whatever Ms. de Vil wants. If I don't, I won't hear the end of it."

"You didn't even take lunch. You deserve a few minutes."

We both know that won't happen as long as the puppy killer is on a rampage.

"Okay, fine." My friend brushes my shoulder. "Call your mom and ask her to watch Jase on Friday night, or I will."

I shake my head. "Sometimes you're a real bitch." My accusation is quiet and accompanied by a big smile.

Sally lifts her chin as her grin grows. "That's why you love me. Don't make me call your mother, because I will. We both agree you deserve a life beyond Jase."

"Are you seriously ganging up on me?"

She doesn't answer.

Before she walks away, I ask, "You mean this Friday night?"

"Yes, just the four of us."

It's only Tuesday. "Give me a day to think about it."

"I'll give you until five o'clock; Brian needs to talk to Pep."

"Bitch," I mutter under my breath as my attention is quickly diverted to the list of things my manager needs done ASAP. Number one: water her plants.

Are you shitting me?

I put myself through college to get a degree in financial planning to water plants?

"Careful," Sally whispers. "You don't want anyone to think you're using my endearment on someone else."

My face snaps upward as I stand and peer about the room of cubicles. Thankfully, no one is looking my way.

"Go. Get out of here. I have work to do. God knows that if I don't, puppies may die."

"Save the puppies and the sexy men," Sally says as she walks away.

My boss's name isn't really de Vil. It's DeVoe.

One evening, not long after I got my job, Sally came over to my apartment. Jase loves her and so do I. She was the one who recommended me for my job. The title, administrative financial assistant, was everything I wanted.

Sometimes ideals and reality don't match.

With Jase in bed, Sally and I talked about work over a bottle —or two—of wine. It was purely a slip of the tongue. I could probably blame it on Jase's obsession with Disney. Nevertheless, instead of DeVoe, de Vil came out—as in Cruella de Vil. Ever since, whenever I'm upset, I imagine Glenn Close and the animated character, and it makes me smile, well, other than the twinge over the puppy coat. That's easier to imagine in cartoon form.

"Amanda."

My neck straightens as my name, accompanied by the click of Christine DeVoe's heels, reaches my ears.

"Amanda, have you received my messages?"

"I have," *all five hundred of them*. I don't say the last part. "I've contacted the purchasing department and Jim is supposed to get back to me. I was waiting until I had an answer. I've sent the emails about the withholdings—"

She nods as her lips come together. As if she were expecting it to be my first priority, she asks, "And what about my plants?"

"They're on my list." *Along with fifty other more important things.* I don't say that part either.

"Don't forget. Phil is looking a little limp."

It takes all of my self-restraint not to burst out laughing. Phil is a large philodendron in her office. However, after the conversation with Sally, a limp Phil has taken on a whole new meaning. "Let me get right on that. The spread sheet for Mr. Smithson can wait."

"Hmm," she murmurs in agreement as she walks away because heaven knows that her plants are more important than the new distribution costs.

Bitch!

I smile as I walk toward her office to get the watering can. This time that title wasn't meant as a term of endearment. That plus the extra toothy smile on Cruella in my imagination adds to keeping my sanity.

A few minutes later back at my desk, my phone rings.

"Hello," I say. "Amanda with Stevens Financial Planning."

"Mrs. Harrison?"

My heart rate triples as I suck in a breath.

When Jackson and I were first married, there was a mix-up with my name change. Someone at some government office checked the wrong box. Though I went by Harrison for two years, it wasn't legal. It was the first year we filed taxes that we discovered the discrepancy. Though I was Harrison in my heart, on paper I wasn't.

At first we laughed about it, saying we knew we were married —that was never questioned—and other than on legal documents, it didn't matter. Like many other plans we had for the future, we thought we would have time to get it all straightened out. With the military, nothing is easy. Jackson went away on deployment sooner than we planned. We figured it could wait. And then, after his death, my life and Jase's were too mixed up. My legal name paled by comparison to other worries on my list of concerns.

Of course, Jase was born with his father's last name. Therefore, though my name was never legally Harrison, I'm only called *Mrs. Harrison* when it has to do with Jase or Jackson.

"Mrs. Harrison?" the woman says again.

"Yes?"

"Ma'am, it's Trisha from ABC Preschool. I'm sorry to bother you, but this is about your son Jason. There was an altercation..."

CHAPTER
Two

Amanda

$\mathcal{M}$y mother hands me a glass of wine as I collapse on the couch in my and Jase's apartment. My son is tucked safely in bed, hardly a scratch on him or the other boy. There may not be a scratch on me either, but I feel like I've gone ten rounds with a heavyweight champion, and I'm fighting a headache from hell.

Looking at the glass of moscato, I debate my options. I could down it all in one swallow and then rub my temples, or I could place the glass on the table, rub my temples, and then drink it all.

First-world problems.

"He's a boy. It's all right," Mom says, forcing me back to reality and more serious concerns.

I continue staring into the glass and swirl the clear liquid. The aroma of fruit fills my senses as the coolness of the glass registers from my fingertips. I tell myself not to cry—to stay strong. It's the same mantra I've been repeating for nearly five years.

"Amanda, your dad talked to Jase. He's a good kid."

My eyes glass over as I look at my mom from under my lashes. "I know. I know he's a good kid, but Dad shouldn't have to be his father and neither should Alec."

Alec is my brother. Even though he lives in a nearby town, he's always willing to help out with Jase. He was the one who gave him his first baseball glove. He's the one Jase wants to emulate. While I'm not sure how I feel about that, I know there could be worse role models for my son.

"Your dad isn't being his father. He's Jase's grandpa and happy to be."

"And being a boy doesn't mean it's all right to fight."

"Of course not," Mom agrees. "Given the situation, I'd hope a girl would do the same thing. I know one who would have."

I take a deep breath. "Times have changed. Fighting is taken more seriously than it used to be. I think the school handled it well, but Jase and the other little boy were wrestling. I didn't wrestle."

"No, but heaven help whomever you were standing up to. You would have knocked them down with your words."

"Jase starts kindergarten in less than a week. I don't want him to be a troublemaker. They aren't as familiar with him at the new school. And there are rules..."

"He isn't a troublemaker. He stood up for what he believes in, just like Jackson did, just like you. You should be proud."

I hate to admit it—to admit that Jase fighting for what he thinks is right makes me proud, but in a way, it does. I remind my mom what I was told when I arrived to the preschool. "The teacher said it started with a talk about the flag. With Labor Day coming up and things, they were talking about patriotism. The other little boy said it was stupid and so are our soldiers. Miss Timmons said she's never seen Jase turn so fast. In a second he was on the other boy."

My mom shrugs. "Your dad told him it was wrong to fight. He also told him it was acceptable to be proud of his daddy."

I nod, swallowing the wine laced with the salt from my tears. Jase, proud of his daddy. That is the same dad who Jase only knows from pictures and stories, the same one who only held his son during a brief furlough before going back to Iraq, before not coming home...

"Besides," my mom says, saving me from my melancholy thoughts, "if Jase is anything like your brother, he and the other little boy are probably best friends again. That's the way boys are."

I fill my lungs, expanding my chest and trying for a cleansing breath.

Mom reaches out and holds my knee. "Honey, Sally called me."

"Shit," I mumble. "I forgot all about her invitation. I don't have time—"

"No, you don't," Mom agrees, interrupting my refusal. "You don't have time to let life pass you by. Jase is a good boy who can stick up for himself. He showed you that today. Now the best thing you can do for him is to work on balance."

I shake my head. "I-I don't want to. Sally said something about me being the right one for this guy. I don't want to find..."

The tears I've been holding back since the call from the preschool spill over my lids. I tilt my face down and once again move the glass to my lips, hoping my mom won't see.

"You're not trying to find *forever*. You're not trying to find *Mr. Right*. However, there is someone who I'd like you to find."

"Who?" I ask, genuinely curious.

"I want you to find Mandy Wells."

My eyes dart her direction. I haven't heard my nickname in conjunction with my maiden name in years, not since Jackson passed away. Mandy was the girl I used to be, the one who loved surprises, believed in forever and happily ever after, and knew that Jackson was my everything and we'd grow old together. "What did you say?"

"You heard me. I remember her." Mom pours more moscato in her glass and tops mine off. "She was a handful, a real pain in the ass." Mom's eyes sparkle. "When you're pregnant, they warn you about boys. Everyone says they get in fights and wrestle, but no one warns you about girls. Sneaky and conniving little things— that's what girls are. That's what Mandy Wells was."

Instead of making me feel worse, her description makes me smile.

"Oh," Mom goes on. "There were days her dad and I thought we'd pull our hair out. One time, more than once actually, she snuck out of her room at night."

"You knew?" I ask in both surprise and embarrassment.

With a knowing grin, she continues, "And when she was with that no-good influence of a friend named Sally..."

Yes, Sally and I have been friends since nearly the beginning of time. It isn't that Sally is or has been a bad influence; it's that we both were. What one of us wouldn't think of, the other would. And despite what my mom is saying, she loves my best friend. She always has.

"...kicked out of a Walmart. I mean, who gets kicked out of Walmart?"

I can't stop my laugh. The ringing tone helps to nudge my headache away. "We weren't doing anything wrong. It wasn't like we were robbing a bank or selling ourselves. We were camping."

"You set up camp in the middle of the camping section."

I recall the scene. "Technically, it was already set up. We just moved in. We were both excited to go camping and then it rained and rained. You, Daddy, and Sally's parents said we couldn't go. You said we'd get sick. Walmart had this cool setup and it was all inside." I lift my glass. "Rather resourceful if you ask me.

"It even had a fake fire made out of orange and yellow crepe paper."

"And you tried to roast marshmallows!"

"Not on the crepe paper," I protest. "They obviously wouldn't have cooked. That's why we used the blowtorch." I take another drink and grin. "It was from their hardware section. They really do have everything there."

Mom shakes her head with a wide smile. "I think the blowtorch may have been your downfall."

"You're probably right. A portable gas grill would have worked better, but we didn't know. Everyone is used to making s'mores on an open flame."

Mom laughs. "When the manager called—"

"We paid for everything first, the marshmallows, graham crackers, and chocolate bars. Even the blowtorch and lighter. We weren't stealing. Who knew a few marshmallows would set off the sprinklers in the entire store? I mean, if the marshmallows hadn't gotten all sticky and gooey and landed on the blowtorch... Really, I think the downfall was the roasting fork. The whole thing was metal and got hot. If you ask me, they should have had better roasting forks. If they had, the entire fire brigade thing could have been avoided."

Mom leans back against the couch and sighs. "I miss her."

"Who?" I ask. "Sally? Because, apparently, you two still talk."

"No, Mandy Wells. I love you, Amanda Jane Wells. I do, but you're twenty-five. You're a great mom, hard worker, wonderful daughter and sister, and a good friend. You deserve to have some fun."

Before I can protest, she goes on, "Don't go out Friday night with Sally and Brian and Brian's friend looking for Mr. Right. Go out with them to have fun, and if you're looking for anyone, look for Mandy Wells."

"I-I can't. Jase starts school..."

"And you're ready. You've been to the school and shown him around. He's met Mrs. Williams, his teacher. He's ecstatic! He has new shoes and clothes. He has a new book bag, pencils, crayons, tablets, pencil case...goodness, that boy has more in that book bag than I do in my desk. It's a wonder he can lift it."

"But he goes to bed—"

"School doesn't start until Tuesday. Friday night, he can stay with us."

"Mom, if I go, I'm not going to be out all night."

"I wasn't suggesting you were. I'm suggesting you might want to stay out past eight." Her brows lift and fall. "The Mandy Wells I knew had trouble with curfews."

I sigh, letting out an exaggerated breath. "Sally said there's something wrong with him."

"The man they want you to meet?" she asks. "Did he murder someone? Is he sick? Is he wanted by the police?"

"Yes, him, but no..." I say, "...nothing like that."

"Again, it's not about him; it's about you."

"Fine. I give up. I can't deal with life while fighting both you and Sally."

My mom's face lights up as small lines form around her eyes. "Do you want to call Sally and tell her, or should I?"

CHAPTER

Amanda

"Mom said you're going on a date," Alec says with a cocky grin.

I quickly turn toward Jase. Thankfully, his attention is focused on our father as they work together to pick the last of Dad's tomatoes. The small garden near the back of the yard is almost done for the season. Many of the earlier producing plants have been harvested and removed.

Jase loves coming over to my parents' and getting dirty with Grandpa. He's always excited when the plants start to grow. My dad starts all of them from seed late in the winter. Then together he and Jase plant them in the tiled ground when the weather starts to warm. It's surprising how much Jase knows about plants at only five years old.

"Shh," I hiss at my brother. "First, she shouldn't have told you, and second, I don't want Jase to hear you."

"What? Jase can't know his mom is a woman?" My brother's eyes open wide. "I mean, I know you don't have much of a rack, but I didn't think that the fact that you're a girl—as in the whole world is either girls or boys—was a secret."

I shake my head. "Jerk," I say lovingly. "The secret is that I'm going out. And it's only one date for one night. It's a blind date. I'm doing it to shut Mom and Sally up."

Alec's laughter roars through our parents' backyard. "Good luck with that. Mom, you might have a chance. But Sally? Nope. She'll never shut up."

That makes me smile. "Point taken."

"I want to hear all about it. You know I need to approve."

My smile fades as heaviness settles on my chest. "Alec, I can't."

My brother reaches out and grabs my hand. His smile wanes a bit as he nods. We're not quite two years apart in age. He's older and was a grade ahead of me in school. He was in the same class as Jackson. That's how Jackson and I became a thing. He was one of Alec's best friends and always around. Jackson went from being a pesky big-brother type to becoming the love of my life. The transition happened so slowly that I can't recall when one ended and the other began. Forever it seemed like we were together, until we weren't.

"I get it," Alec says. "You think that I don't think about him. When the other guys and I are playing softball, or hanging out at Wayne's Place after a game, sometimes I think of him and how none of it is fair. Jackson should be there with us. Hell, we lost the game the other night because Stivey couldn't catch a fly ball that sailed all the way back to the fence. My first thought was that Jackson should have been playing left field."

Swallowing back my tears, I smile. "He liked outfield, especially left, so he could show off his arm."

"Shit! He had an arm. I can still feel the burn through my glove when he'd put some speed behind it."

"This is different."

Alec turns to make sure Dad and Jase are still occupied. When he turns back, he shrugs. "It is, but it isn't. I wasn't married to the guy, but I loved him." He softly punches my arm. "Don't make me get all sentimental. The thing is that Jackson knew the risk for his service. I knew the risk. We all did when we were there. He died loving what he was doing. He was so happy about Jase and being a dad. And he was proud to be a soldier. He was living. He wouldn't want you to stop."

A lone tear leaks from the corner of my eye. "I hate you."

Alec smiles. "Yeah, sis, I hate you too. Have fun."

"Why did Mom even tell you?"

"Because Dad's bringing Jase to my softball game Friday night."

"He is—"

"Mom!" Jase yells as he comes running toward us with a big red tomato in his grasp. "Look at this giant to-mado."

"It's big," I agree.

"As big as a softball," Alec says as he kneels down to Jase's height.

"Uncle Alec, Grandpa said we're going to see you play ball Friday night." Jase then turns to me and his blue eyes open wide. "Mom, are you coming too?"

That familiar ache settles in my chest. I don't like to be away from him.

"No way," Alec answers before I can. "It's a guy thing. Just you, Grandpa, and me."

"Really? A *guy thing*!" My son is practically bouncing with each word. No. Jase *is* bouncing as his grip on the tomato tightens.

"Hey buddy," I say. "Why don't you give me that tomato before you squeeze it and it busts wide open?"

He hands me the tomato and tilts his head. "Am I strong enough to break it?"

"You are."

"Like Uncle Alec," Jase says as he flexes his tiny arm, seeing a muscle that's barely there. Then his smile dims. "Mom, is it okay if I do a guy night? Will you miss me?"

"I will, but I'll be okay, but what about Grandma?"

"Oh, she's meeting us for ice cream after," Alec volunteers. "At Roy's."

As he completes the word *cream*, Jase is off running toward the house and shouting for his grandma. All I can catch is that they're going to Roy's and not the concession stand.

"See, Jase is going to have fun Friday night. You should too."

I let out a deep breath. "What about you? When are you going to settle down with one lucky lady?"

My brother puffs out his chest. "That's the thing. There's no way to keep all this man with just one lady. It would obviously be too much for one woman to handle."

I laugh. "Yes, that is the rumor on the street."

"Because many have tried. You know, it really wouldn't be fair to the ladies of this here city..." He leans back even farther. "Or state...hell, country. Alec Wells is not the tying-down kind."

My hand flies up as I scrunch my brow. "Okay, bro. More information than your sister needs to hear."

His lips quirk in an uneven smirk. "That wasn't what I meant..."

"Yes, watch what *guy things* you share with Jase on Friday night."

"Don't worry about that. Uncle Alec will teach him how to be a girl magnet. Seriously, kindergarten is where it starts. I'll set him straight on ponytails and dimples. I'll give him the lowdown on all the important stuff. Rule number one: stay away from drugs and girls who eat paste."

As I turn and look out over the yard, I gently toss the tomato from one hand to the other. "Do you ever think of doing something totally out of character?"

Alec snorts. "Amanda, this is me. All the time!"

"Yeah, right. I'm just not sure I can."

"Hold on," he says as he rushes away toward the garage. When he comes back he has his softball bag, the one he keeps in the trunk of his car. Unzipping the bag, Alec pulls out an aluminum bat and pushes it my direction. "Trade me for the tomato."

My gaze narrows. "Why?"

"Out of character, sis. You can do it."

"Are you kidding? Look at this..." I hold it up. "...it's big and juicy. I could make a great salad for lunch tomorrow at work."

"Which is in character, or you could live a little."

Slowly, I hand him the softball-sized tomato and reach for the bat.

Walking backward and palming the tomato, Alec lowers his voice to the tone we used as kids when we were planning secrets from our parents. "You'll only have one chance. Don't blow it."

I shift my feet to the side, bend my knees, and after adjusting my hands, lift the bat in the air.

"You ready?" Alec asks as he moves to a pitcher's stance.

"What if I miss? I haven't played in years."

He winks. "It's like riding a bike."

"How can everything be like riding a bike?"

"Everything is. Now, watch me. Keep your eye on the ball."

"It's a tomato."

His arm moves, a nice controlled underhand pitch. As the fruit flies toward me, I hear Jase and my mother yell at the same time.

"Mom?"

"Amanda!"

I pull the bat back and swing. The connection happens with a *thud*. All at once, the air fills with seeds, and tomato juice rains down.

"What in the world?" Mom asks.

"That was so cool. Can I try?" Jase asks as he gets closer. "Mom, you have sprinkles all over you."

I look down at the red droplets and small seeds splattered over my blouse. As I hand the messy bat back to my brother, I wipe more tomato remnants from my cheeks.

Mom's head is moving back and forth as she takes in the scene. "What are you two doing? And here I thought I had grown children."

"Don't give her a hard time," Alec says. "She was just—"

Before he can finish, I interrupt. "Looking for someone."

Mom's smile grows and she nods approvingly. "I think she's closer than she was yesterday."

"Can I hit a tomato?" Jase asks, bouncing on the tips of his toes. "Can I?"

Alec looks my direction.

"Do you want to get sprinkles?" I ask.

Jase's head bobs up and down.

Mom waves her hand. "I don't care. But only one. I'd like to get a chance to eat some of those."

"Sure," I say to both Jase and Alec. "Out of character." Next, I turn to Jase. "You have to hit it the first time. If you miss, it will probably break."

"I can do it," he says, lifting the too-big bat.

"And then it's home for a bath. No sleeping with sprinkles."

"Oh, Mom!" Jase and Alec whine at the same time just before a new tomato sails through the air.

Thud!

My mom and I laugh as Jase turns our way with a big grin and covered in red polka dots.

CHAPTER
Four

Mandy

I can't believe how nervous I am. I thought I gave up being nervous years ago, but here I am, my palms moist, pulse accelerated, and breath shallow. Despite the air conditioning and overhead fans, a bead of perspiration drips down the center of my back while another one trickles between my breasts.

Out of character.

That's what this all is, and I'm not sure how I feel about it. I know my son isn't missing me. He's been excited about his *guy night* ever since his uncle presented it to him. I do think Mom was slightly put off, but she assured me that it was fine. Her plans include enjoying a little peace and quiet until ice cream time. Then she'll be plenty busy with sticky fingers and a sugar buzz at bath time.

Stepping farther into the restaurant's entry, I take one last glance down at my blue sundress and heeled sandals. Peeking from the tips of the sandals are brightly painted toenails. As I take one last look, the realization hits me: I haven't primped for a date since Jackson. I haven't worried about how I look or how I style my hair. I mean, I look professional for work, but other than that, it's just me, Jase, my parents, and sometimes Alec or Sally. I'm the mom at Little League with the baseball cap, T-shirt, and ponytail. I'm the lady at the grocery store with no makeup on and probably wearing Jase's peanut butter smears as an accessory.

Thinking about the preparation I put into tonight, I fight the urge to rush to the restroom. If I do, will it be to make sure it's me in the mirror, touch up my seldom-worn lip gloss, or throw up?

Deep breath.

Inhale and exhale.

If I do go to the restroom, who will I see? Will it be me, or the Mandy Wells my mom wants me to find? My lips quirk to a sideways smile—a lot like my brother's—as I recall the tomato seeds I washed from my hair the other night.

If I can smash a giant tomato to smithereens, maybe I can do this. No. I can. I can sit and make conversation. After all, I won't be alone with this friend of Brian's; I'll have Sally and Brian there with me.

As my confidence grows, so do my insecurities.

Questions bloom, sprouting new questions.

Do I know what I'm I doing?

What do I even know about this guy?

I run the facts through my head. Brian and Sally call him Pep. What kind of name is that? He's Brian's age, late twenties or early thirties, never married, and an ex-professional hockey player. What does ex mean? It means he no longer plays hockey, but what does he do? Is he unemployed?

Do I care?

Brian's an ex-hockey player and he's employed. Does it matter?

"Table, ma'am?" the very young-looking girl behind the hostess stand asks.

When did I become a *ma'am*?

"No. Not yet. I'm meeting some friends."

The girl motions to the archway. "You can wait in the bar if you'd like."

I nod. Trying to swallow my worries, I turn and step that way.

My mind continues to churn.

Why does it matter if he's employed? This isn't a job interview. I don't need his resume.

I don't.

But maybe a police background check and a medical clearance would be nice. I start to make a mental checklist.

Background check.

Medical records.

Wait! I don't plan to take this night to anywhere that would require medical records. Then again, better safe than sorry. I mean, what if those performance-enhancing drugs did more than affect the circulation in certain parts of his body? What other side effects do they have? Do I care?

Taking another deep breath, I stand for a moment on the other side of the archway as my eyes adjust to the dimly lit bar. It's a popular establishment and busy. And while it's what my dad would call a safe location for meeting a stranger, it's also far enough away from home that it's not full of nosy, well-meaning friends.

I scan the room, looking for Sally and Brian. Of course, I can't find them.

From glancing at the clock in my car before I was brave enough to enter, I know that I'm early. A giggle makes my throat clench as I shake my head. Sally has never been early in her life. She usually makes it to work on time, but that's by the skin of her teeth.

Being early is a chronic ailment with me. With Jackson having been in the military, late was unacceptable and on time was considered late. The only possible arrival time was early. It's one of the habits I can't seem to break.

Since Sally and Brian aren't here yet, I look for an available seat. I want a place to wait and fade into the background. If maybe I could avoid looking quite so conspicuous, that would be a plus too.

A table alone would fail at the inconspicuous part. Therefore, I decide to make my way up to the bar, all the while doing my best to exude confidence—though it's fake. As I do, my pulse increases with the realization that I've never been to a bar by myself. Jackson and I married at nineteen. I had just turned twenty-one when...

I work again to fill my lungs and hope that no one notices my shaking hands or stuttered steps. Being that it's a Friday night, there are only a few empty barstools and of course, none with more space than a single. Quietly, I ease onto one stool wedged between two people and wonder for at least the tenth time if everyone can sense how tense I am.

I shoot Sally a text: *I'm here. Where are you?*

"Drink, pretty lady?"

I look up and try to stop myself from cringing at the bartender's greeting. It isn't his words that creep me out, but the leer as his eyes move from my face to my breasts and finally back to my eyes.

"U-um, yes, a glass of white moscato."

When his gaze lingers a little too long, I look away and stare at my phone, hoping that my focus on the screen will accelerate Sally's answer. Yeah, right. As my mom would say, a watched pot never boils.

"Sorry, some men are jerks."

I lift my eyes to the deep voice sitting beside me. I hadn't even noticed him when I sat, other than that he was there. Now as I'm staring into his eyes, I'm wondering how I hadn't.

I blink. Once. Twice. I'm trying to decide if this man is talking to me and if I remember how to respond.

Sapphire-blue eyes from beneath a protruding brow and wavy dark-brown hair have suddenly stolen my ability to speak. As I try to swallow, my gaze lowers, scanning his narrow nose, full lips, and chiseled jaw. I inhale, taking in how his jawline contains just the right amount of beard—trimmed yet soft. Even though I haven't even seen his body, my insides are twisting like they haven't in years.

This is ridiculous. I'm not some eighteen-year-old schoolgirl.

It's then I realize that his broad shoulder infringes upon my personal space and that our bodies are nearly touching.

Silently, I nod, agreeing with his statement that men are jerks and trying to remember how to speak. "I-it's okay." The words finally find their way off my tongue. "I'm just a little nervous. My friend is supposed to meet me."

The man turns my way, his shoulder brushing mine. "Your friend should never leave you alone with these wolves. He doesn't sound like much of a friend."

Mr. Blue-eyes extends his large hand. "Hello, I'm—"

"Hey beautiful," the bartender interrupts. "Here's your wine."

Blue-eyes turns to the bartender. "She's with me. While I agree she's beautiful, *Miss* is an acceptable greeting."

Suddenly, all the menacing glances from the bartender disappear.

"Hey, sorry. I didn't know."

"I don't care if you knew or not. Serving drinks is your job— not hitting on every gorgeous woman."

Beautiful? Gorgeous?

I'm speechless as Mr. Blue-eyes sends the bartender away looking less like a predator and more like a wounded puppy with his tail between his legs.

Once he's gone, I smirk, my cheeks filling with heat. "Thank you. You didn't need to do that."

His shoulder moves against mine again as he shrugs. "I didn't need to, but I've been watching him. He's a snake." Blue-eyes turns my way. "And thank you."

"Me?"

"Yes, thanks for letting me say that. I wasn't insinuating you couldn't handle yourself. It's just that he's been pulling those moves on every woman since I arrived, and I was dying to put him in his place. Really, you did me a favor."

My cheeks rise as I lift my glass of wine. "Well, you're welcome." I propose a toast. "To righting the world of wrongs."

We clink glasses—my wine against his tall glass of beer—as he chuckles. Like his voice, his laugh is deep and sends vibrations from my ears throughout my entire body, down my chest, my tummy, and lower. I swear my toes tingle from his laughter.

As I take a sip, my phone pings. I read the text and sigh.

"Don't tell me your friend is standing you up?" he asks.

I shake my head. "No, she's on her way. But she's running late. Surprise. Surprise."

"Oh, *she*? I assumed..."

Heat floods my system. *Shit*—maybe I shouldn't have said that. What if this guy is a serial killer or something? Then again, maybe it's the way my bare shoulder rests against his sleeve-covered one or the way his warmth radiates from under the cotton.

"Yes, she," I confirm. "But she's not alone. She talked me into..." I lift my glass again to my lips. "Never mind, I'm sure you have better things to do than to listen to me and my plans for the evening."

The tips of his grin curl upward, making his cheeks rise and small lines form near the corners of his eyes. There's something about his smile that has me mesmerized.

"Honestly, I've been dreading this night. Listening to you is much better than what I had planned."

"Oh, wait. Am I stopping your plans? I'm sorry."

"No," he protests. "I know this sounds cliché, but I'm supposed to be meeting someone also, and so far, I'm alone."

The small amount of wine I've consumed courses through my bloodstream, giving me a boost of courage and reminding me of the *Mandy* my mom wanted me to find. I unashamedly scan Blue-eyes up and down. Due to the bar, I can't see below his waist, but the way the buttons on his green Oxford shirt strain over his chest, I can tell he's fit. The waist of his slacks is trim. "Admittedly, it's been a long time for me, but I honestly can't imagine anyone standing you up."

His cheeks blush in an endearing way as he returns my scan. "I can most definitely say the same thing about you."

He nods toward the side of the bar as two people vacate a booth along the wall. "How about we move over there until our respective friends arrive?"

Taking a deep breath, I look back at the screen of my phone. There's nothing new from Sally, just her last message saying there was something happening with Brian's work, but that soon they'll be on their way.

Part of me wants to forget the whole thing, pay for my wine, and go home, but there is another part—the part that took the first step out of character, the one who bought a new dress and shoes and painted her toenails, the one who worried about her hair and makeup, and the one who was just called *beautiful* and *gorgeous* by a very handsome man—who wants to stay. Besides, what if Brian's friend is a sleazebag, like the bartender? At least spending a few minutes with this guy would save the evening.

Not waiting for my answer, Mr. Blue-eyes stands. As he lays cash on the bar, he extends his hand my direction. "Shall we?"

His movement fills my senses with the scent of his cologne. It's spicy. In one whiff, the aroma is fixed in my memory. My eyes drift to the floor, and slowly my gaze moves upward. From his shiny shoes and trim pleated trousers, to the belt accentuating his waist, and up to the V of his chest covered by the light-green shirt, I take it all in. I'd seen most of it when he was sitting, but the view is even better when he stands.

I swallow and slowly place my hand in the palm of his. The way his fingers envelop mine suddenly makes me feel small, such a contrast to Jase. When I stand, this man is easily six inches taller than I, even in my new heels.

"Only until my friends arrive," I clarify, hoping to give myself an escape plan if needed.

"Agreed."

The booth is a half circle. I slide in first with him beside me. Once we settle, I miss the warmth of his shoulder.

CHAPTER
Five

J don't even know her name, but I want to know so much more. Why was she nervous when she first sat down? Her shoulder trembled against mine as that dick of a bartender threw his cheesy lines her way.

For a moment, she seemed meek as a church mouse, but then something changed. She's different—a contradiction. When she looks directly at me, there's strength and determination behind her beautiful light-blue eyes. I'm fascinated by the color. If the world were to be divided into three eye colors, blue, brown, and green, we'd have the same. Yet they aren't. Hers are much different, lighter. They're a soft pastel like the hue of the horizon just before the sun rises.

As we settle in the booth, I wonder who in their right mind would stand this lady up. Her friend is an asshole, even if she is a woman. Obviously, this beautiful lady isn't accustomed to being out and about by herself.

What does that mean?

I've scanned her petite frame more than once. She isn't wearing a wedding ring. Maybe she's just out of a relationship. Maybe she's not used to going to bars alone.

I chastise myself. I'm supposed to be on a blind date—the first date I've had since I moved here to start my new life. I'm supposed to be leaving the pickup-artist side of me in Florida.

This is crazy. I can't understand why this blue-eyed brunette has me so enthralled. I didn't even want to go on the blind date. I'm not looking for a one-night stand or a relationship. I'm at this bar because my old teammate made it sound like I was doing his girlfriend a favor. Her friend needs to be eased back into the world of dating.

I laugh at the thought of me easing someone into dating. The old Malcolm, the one Brian knew, was all about getting laid and moving on. Maybe that's what Brian wanted me to do, pop the woman's dating cherry.

That isn't who I am anymore. That Malcolm hung up his skates and retired. I left him in Florida.

It's all too easy to score in the sunshine state. Women walk around half-naked everywhere you go. It isn't just the beaches. It's the grocery stores and the movie theaters. I don't know how clothing stores don't go out of business down there.

And the women who throw themselves at hockey players—at all pro athletes—are obnoxious and plentiful. If I were a gentleman, I could say I never took advantage, but after a game when the adrenaline is pumping, the best-known cure for blowing off steam is thrusting in and out of a warm, willing pussy—full-body aerobics with benefits.

Those days are over. I'm no longer Pep—I'm Malcolm Peppernick. I'm not a player—in any sense of the word. I'm responsible. This new city and new career are supposed to cement that.

Her phone pings.

As she looks at it, I think about my old nickname, Pep. It came as a result of my energy on the ice and because it's short for my last name. All it took was for a few broadcasters to use it and boom, it stuck. That is how it started, but with time it meant more. According to rumors, my pep was for more than hockey. They said I had pep in the sack too. Well, not always a bed. A bar bathroom. The hallway outside the locker room. The truth is that women like to talk as much as men. Those bimbos following the team had their own belts filled with notches. If one woman said I gave her two orgasms, the next one said I gave her three.

At the time, my concentration wasn't on counting their

climaxes. It was more on my own gratification. As long as the rumors flew, there were plenty of opportunities and willing participants to satisfy my own needs. I may have used a few of those women, but it was a two-way street, and besides, they weren't complaining.

All of that is history.

That part of me is gone. Over the years, I left hockey behind. I had a good career, but it takes its toll on the body. I wanted something more. I went back to school and have dedicated myself to a rewarding career, one that is not conducive to a playboy lifestyle. I rethought my priorities and am happy about it. Right now, a woman or even contentment isn't on my list of goals. Getting my new career up and running is.

Nevertheless, as much as I want to fight it, I can't deny my attraction for this beautiful woman. What I can deny is wanting to use her. Maybe it's because in the very short time since we've met, I can tell that she's totally different than the hockey groupies who used to throw themselves at me.

There's something about her. As she frowns at the screen of her phone, I want to know more. I want to know her as I've never wanted to know anyone before.

What makes this blue-eyed beauty tick?

Watching her pink lower lip disappear behind her white teeth, I wonder what she's thinking. At the same time, I miss how close we were at the bar. I miss the sensation of her shoulder against mine.

When she looks back up, she says, "Thank you, but you didn't need to buy my drink."

I just smile. It's not her sweet voice that makes me happy, though the sound of it is like a melody. It's the way she appears to have relaxed. We're too far apart to touch, but by the calm liquid in her glass, I can tell her trembling from before has stopped.

"You can get the next round," I offer.

Her long lashes flutter over her eyes as pink fills her cheeks.

"I-I probably should go. This was supposed to be...well, my friend just texted again. Her boyfriend has a work emergency. She can't make it, so the blind date is off. I guess my night is a bust."

I lean closer. "On the contrary, you, beautiful lady, owe me a drink. You can't leave with a debt unpaid."

Her smile grows. "Then I better pay up."

"Do you always fulfill all your obligations?"

She nods, making her dark hair move and flow in long waves over her shoulders. "Always."

"Tell me something about you," I pry, wanting to know it all.

"Tonight was supposed to be my reintroduction into learning how to have fun. I guess it fizzled."

I reach out. As the tips of my fingers contact the warmth of her arm, I pause. Our connection sizzles and crackles. It's so strong I can practically hear it over the din of the bar. When I look up, I wonder if she's feeling the same thing. Her eyes are wide, but just as quickly the long lashes veil her true thoughts.

Whether she sensed it or not, I'm pleased that she doesn't pull away.

"I don't know about you, but neither *fizzle* nor *bust* is a word I'd use to describe my night." I continue, "Like I said, I was dreading this evening. That isn't a pickup line. I was supposed to meet a friend here, a person I knew a long time ago, a person who knew me a long time ago. I recently moved to town and other than work, I've been kind of a hermit. My friend and I were close once, but until recently I hadn't seen him in years. I've changed a lot since then." I shrug. "I'm not sure if he understands that about me...he wanted me to meet someone nice who he knows." I cringe. "You know how blind dates can be?"

She shakes her head.

"You don't?"

"No." The word comes out more as a sigh. "I've never officially been on one."

"Consider yourself lucky. They never pan out. When someone is described as *nice*, that's code for uglier than shit. I'm a little afraid to look around in case there's a nice woman looking for me."

Her laughter fills the booth as she shrugs. "Tonight was supposed to be my first." Her eyes spring open wide as she clarifies, "My first *blind date*. But, well, my friend warned me that the guy has issues."

"Ew." My nose scrunches. "That's even worse. You didn't get the nice guy speech?"

"I think she was taking it easy on me. You know, easing me in slowly."

I scoot closer and nudge my shoulder against hers. "Go ahead. Spill. What is the guy's problem?"

Her head moves rapidly back and forth. "I-I haven't had enough wine for that."

It's all the encouragement I need. My hand flies into the air catching the waitress's attention. "Two more drinks and..." I look my companion's way. "...menus?"

There's but a second of hesitation. "Yes," she says, "but I'm buying my own meal."

"You heard the lady," I say to the waitress. "Menus and she's buying."

"I-I..."

I've officially fallen for her little stutter. If I have her pegged correctly, it comes right before a burst of confidence.

"Sure," she proclaims. "Why the hell not?"

Bingo!

"I plan to learn the issues with the guy you were supposed to meet before the night is through."

"I plan to learn your name."

I lean back. How do I not know her name and yet the conversation has been anything but uncomfortable? It's been fun and relaxed.

I extend my hand and she takes it. "Malcolm Peppernick, and you?"

"Mandy," she says with a grin. "Mandy Wells."

Her hand lingers in mine. It's just like before: when helping her from her chair, I touched her arm and there was a pull—a magnetic force drawing me closer to her.

Still holding her hand, my gaze goes to her lips. They're pink and plump. The shimmer is light and not obnoxious. It's like the hint of perfume that lingers around Mandy: sweet while not overpowering but still incredibly intoxicating.

My willpower is waning by the second as I move even closer. I want to taste her lips and probe her warm mouth. I want to capture the lingering sips of wine and drink them down.

Instead of pulling away, she allows her gaze to follow suit, dropping to my lips, intent on watching their next move.

It's when her tongue darts to the surface that I know I can't let this pass. I lean toward her. "Mandy, I want to kiss you."

She doesn't say yes, and she doesn't say no.

Another inch and our lips unite. I capture hers, tasting her shiny gloss as we kiss. It's the first kiss I've experienced in months, and I'm instantly a man deprived, wanting more—no, needing more.

Like lightning to a dry grassy field, as our breath mingles, a fire ignites, rushing through me straight from my lips to my dick. It too has been on hiatus. No longer. Like Frankenstein's lifeless body, Mandy's bolt of lightning zaps my cock back to life. First with a twitch, but as our kiss lingers, it is growing by the second.

This beautiful lady is the power and energy I hadn't realized I was missing.

The restaurant disappears as we move closer, the front of her dress brushing against my chest. I reach for her arms, turning her until both of her perfect tits are smashed against me, until nothing but our clothes separates us.

CHAPTER
Six

Mandy

y nipples harden to painful nubs as they flatten against Malcolm's hard chest.

Words aren't forming. They've been replaced with moans and whimpers as I squirm against the seat.

Who the hell am I? What is happening?

As heat and wetness flood my core, I contemplate how I went from nun to slut in a matter of forty minutes. This isn't the Amanda Wells my mother knows: the responsible mother and daughter, the hard worker and caring sister, the good friend.

Who is this?

I know the answer. This is a grown woman who's been held captive in life and sees a chance for a small reprieve.

No—not sees. This is a woman who *feels* that reprieve with everything in her.

I push the thoughts of everyday life from my mind. I can't think about the person I usually am. If I did, I'd feel a responsibility to ask Sally if Brian's friend is here. I don't want to. I want to live in the now.

I do.

I let all of that fade from my thoughts as I surrender to the sensations of this man: his masculine scent, the warmth of his embrace, and the heat from his hardening body.

This is only one night: I mentally repeat the promise I made to my mom and Sally. Granted, it's becoming more difficult to hear over the swish of my blood coursing through my veins. But as our lips continue their dance, I decide to follow through on that promise. For just this one night, I'm going to let myself live.

Malcolm's heat consumes me, causing my body to melt in his grasp. Our hearts beat wildly against the other's as they pound out the rhythm of a song I'd forgotten. I relish his touch as his large hands skirt over my exposed arms. No longer foreign, his contact ignites sparks. The small hairs on my skin stand to attention as if waiting for lightning to strike. His fingers brush against the side of my breast.

I push closer, wanting more.

My mind and body battle.

My mind screams its instructions: move away and protest. But instead, my body rebels, liquefying at his touch and longing for more.

His lips bruise mine as his tongue probes their seam. Willingly, I open, gasping for breath as the lingering taste of beer mixes with my wine. The blend scorches my blood as his closeness sends the boiling fluid to forgotten parts of my body. I whimper as my insides painfully clench, and my thighs press tightly together.

Though I want to hide my reaction to his kiss, to his touch...I fear I don't.

What I really want to do is push my hips closer and allow more of our bodies to touch. It's been so long since I've felt this way, so long since I've wanted...really wanted.

Malcolm's spicy scent surrounds me as it merges with musk. Suddenly, I'm blinded in his cloud.

When we finally pull apart, before I can speak or even contemplate what happened, Malcolm's blue eyes shine down on me, taking me in and reading me.

His voice rumbles through the background commotion of the bar. "You taste like sweet wine and smell like perfume and desire."

Warmth fills my cheeks. "You taste like good beer."

"Good? You're a beer connoisseur?"

I shrug. "Mostly, I know cheap beer."

He lifts my chin, bringing his indigo eyes into focus. The room disappears, making those blue orbs all I can see.

"I'm a connoisseur," he says as his thumb gently rubs over my bruised lips. "And you, beautiful Mandy, if you were a beer, would never be a cheap one. No, you're a rich custom craft brew. I see it in your eyes, feel it in your touch, and smell it in the air. Kissing a stranger isn't something you do, is it?"

I try to move my eyes away, but Malcolm's grip of my chin is unrelenting. Meeting his gaze, I reply, "No. I won't even bore you with how long it's been since I've kissed a real man."

His eyes sparkle. "You kiss fake men?"

"Boys. Well, only one actually."

"You kiss boys..." And then, as if the reality of his statement hits home, he asks, "You have a son?"

My heart flutters, its speed increasing by the second. "I do, but I don't want to talk about him. Not because he isn't important for he is—he's my world—but because tonight isn't about him. It's about me." I can't gauge Malcolm's reaction. I can only guess that he's assuming that I'm some needy woman trying to get a man to take on the responsibility of a kid who isn't his.

I reach out and splay my fingers over his chest. His heart is beating to match mine. "I don't want to talk about him," I continue, "because he'll never know about you—I'll never tell him and never introduce you. Don't worry. I'm not after a man to rescue me. I'm perfectly content with my life as a mother. I just wanted to remember what it felt like to be a woman...for just one night."

"I'm not anti-children—"

I shake my head. "Stop. That doesn't matter." It's then that I notice the filled glasses on the table and laugh. "When did the waitress come?"

Malcolm bows his head until our noses touch. He inhales

deeply, his eyes closing as his hand falls to my lap. "I'd say just after you."

More heat floods my cheeks. "I-I didn't..."

"Then we need to do something about that." He looks again at the full glasses. "I think the drinks came while my tongue was busy getting to know your sweet mouth." His hand splays over my thigh.

My breathing hitches. "Malcolm?"

"You said you want one night. One night doesn't end with a kiss. It begins with one."

Ignoring his lingering touch, I reach for my menu. As I do, Malcolm lifts my glass of wine with his free hand and brings it to my lips. "Drink, beautiful Mandy. You have secrets to spill, and we only have one night to do it."

I sip the sweet, fruity liquid, its alcohol going straight to my head. Or is it the kiss, the closeness, or just Malcolm?

"You know," I say as I turn his direction, "I had a blind date tonight with a man with issues. The poor guy may be here somewhere, and I'm standing him up."

Malcolm's fingers move higher up my thigh as he shrugs. "Poor shmuck. His issues will probably get worse."

"I'm not sure I can handle that responsibility."

Malcolm laughs. "So you're saying that you wish you were with that guy?"

I don't have to think to respond—not that I could with his fingers moving closer to my arousal. I don't want to be anywhere —not with Sally and Brian, not with their friend Pep. For the first time since, well, for too long, I feel alive. I'm with the person fate intended and I'm not complaining. "No. I think fate had other plans, and who am I to argue with fate."

His fingers move below the hem of my dress.

"One night," he whispers.

My thighs part as I suck in a ragged breath. As he brushes the crotch of my panties, the choices on the menu blur. Though my hunger grows, food no longer seems important.

Malcolm speaks softly near my neck. His warm breath is the breeze rekindling the earlier blaze as his fingers stroke the flame. "Do you see anything you want?"

My body is on fire as I writhe toward his touch. I turn until our eyes meet, purposely allowing my legs to fall open farther to his desires. "Yes, I do see what I want."

"Me too and it's not on that menu. Since we only have one night, how about we both stand up our blind dates and make other plans?"

My breasts throb in anticipation as I try to take a breath. My words come out as a sigh. "W-what would those plans be?"

"I have wine and beer at my apartment and a pizza app on my phone. How about we leave this crowded place?"

My heart beats out of my chest as my mouth threatens to sabotage my one night. I made a commitment to Brian's friend. The crowd is supposed to be my safety net, but as Malcolm's touch lingers, I decide to live for me. One night. "I-I..."

"If you spread those sexy thighs wider, we could finish what we started. We can do that here in front of this entire restaurant or back at my place." He nips my ear, the jolt zapping straight to where his fingers are roaming.

Fuck!

"I promise you'll come."

My insides tighten. I haven't been so turned on in years. "Malcolm..."

"Fate, Mandy, fate."

"Who am I to argue with fate? Besides," I say with a grin, "I do love pizza."

Before I can comprehend that I just agreed to go to his apartment, Malcolm removes his hand, bringing his fingers to his nose and inhales with a cocky smile. "So close."

I want to argue, but what's the point?

Malcolm pulls more bills from his wallet and lays them on the table.

"Um, I was supposed to pay for that."

His eyes shimmer. "Oh, beautiful, if tonight goes as I hope, you'll repay me many times."

CHAPTER
Seven

Mandy

While I was driving, the thought occurred to me many times to stop following Malcolm's car and head home. Though the thoughts came and went, I didn't.

Like the gentleman he is, after I park beside his car, he opens my door, takes my hand, and leads me to his apartment. We chat pleasantly about the weather as the fireflies flicker in the darkness. Up the stairs and down the hall, we manage small talk. However, once the door to his apartment is barely closed, all pretense is lost.

I'm back in Malcolm's arms, surrounded by his spicy-scented embrace. The musk of our desire, my perfume, and his cologne combine in an all-encompassing vapor, an intoxicating potion that dazes and excites me. It fills my senses like a drug and suddenly, I'm an addict.

Though my mind wants to protest, my body is more energized than it's been in years. Zeal surges through me—all the way from my tingly scalp to my curling toes and everywhere in between. His full, sensual lips are on mine. His muscled body is pressed against me. I'm sandwiched between him and the wall, and the way I'm pushing back, I chose him.

My moans fill the air, breaking through the fog of desire as he reaches for my behind and lifts me effortlessly as if I'm merely a feather in his arms. My legs surround his waist and my ankles lock together. The dress I worked so hard to find is bunched around my waist, exposing my underwear. Shamelessly, I grind against his hardness, relishing the friction. In no time, the straps of my dress are lowered exposing my bra. Long, thick fingers push the lace down. The air fills with his hiss as my breasts overflow the cups.

Every part of me is alive. My nipples pebble as the erection beneath me grows. I let out a suppressed whimper as his rod of steel moves against my panties. I'm a jumble of emotions: desire and fear, excitement and uncertainty. My senses are on high alert, feeling everything at once.

"Mandy, I want to be inside you." Malcolm's desire comes out as less of a question and more of a demand.

My pussy clenches as I imagine the rod that is teasing my covered clit thrusting inside me.

I nod as I try to breathe and concentrate on desire. One night. My voice is strong. "I want that too."

With my arms around his neck and my forehead against his solid chest, he reaches for my panties and moves the crotch to the side, slipping one finger and then two deep inside me. My head rolls backward as I gasp and relish the sensation.

"You're so fucking wet," he hisses as his fingers move, orchestrating magic.

Consumed with need, my entire body moves to his rhythm, up and down as both fingers curl and his thumb brushes my clit. Every nerve within me sizzles as Malcolm brings me to the edge of my figurative cliff; below me is a raging wildfire, and I'm ready to take the plunge.

"O-oh." My sounds aren't words but primitive noises as my muscles tighten.

I gasp as he takes away the pleasure, but then all at once, my heartbeat quickens at his next move. Severing our kisses, Malcolm brings his fingers to our lips and plunges them inside his mouth and over his tongue. Butterflies of uncertainty morph to bats of wanton lust as his blue eyes sparkle in the still-dim apartment, and he pulls his fingers from his lips and teases mine.

Without hesitation, I open, allowing his fingers inside, tasting the sweetness of his kiss combined with the tanginess of my own essence. Approvingly, his eyes shine as I suck one of his fingers and then both.

"Fuck," he growls as his hips resume their grind.

Again, he reaches for my panties. "I hope you're not particularly attached to these."

Before I can respond, the ripped fabric falls from my waist. Lowering me to the ground, he reaches for his wallet. As I kick off my heeled sandals, I can't stop my eyes from watching his every move as he undoes his belt and trousers and frees his impressive penis. My lip disappears behind my teeth as I take in his length and girth. His pants slide down his wide thighs but my attention is on his hands. I hear the sounds of my own wanton moans as he quickly sheaths the stretched skin. And then all at once, I'm back in his arms.

Time forgets to move and my breathing hitches. My tummy muscles tense as I wrap my arms tighter around his thick neck, secure my legs around his waist, and lift myself higher. In that moment, I'm well aware that I'm completely exposed to his impending invasion, and I can't think of anywhere I'd rather be.

"Mandy, are you sure?" his deep, reassuring tone asks.

I nod, unsure why I want this man as much as I do, why I'm so attracted.

He leans back, making sure our gazes meet. In his eyes, I see both determination and desire. He wants a verbal answer, yet words aren't currently within my ability. Instead, with the wall behind me and Malcolm supporting me, I reach down and fist his cock.

"F-fuck." His word rumbles through the air in multiple syllables.

I grasp his length as low as I can reach and run my hand up and down. Enjoying the width and length that I'd only briefly seen, I stroke the sheathed skin and run my thumb over the tip. I know that safety is best, yet I find myself wishing I could touch the slickness of his cum as he had mine.

His head falls backward as I direct his cock to my willing, wet pussy.

A scream escapes my lips as he plunges deep inside me.

Fuck! He's so large.

It takes multiple thrusts and wiggles as I stretch underused muscles and work to accommodate his girth. Each time is deeper than the last, each one extracting my whimpers of pleasure. I can't remember ever feeling so full, so extended. Up and down I ride until he is fully inside of me. Lunge after lunge, he drives into me, each thrust finding new points of ecstasy as my fingers clench his shoulders and fingernails threaten his shirt. Wanting to be closer, I reach for his hair, weaving and gripping until I've pulled his mouth to my neck.

I want all of this man, his cock buried inside me, his beard against my sensitive skin, and his warm breath panting in my ear.

All at once, my toes curl and body goes rigid.

Noises like I've never made scream from the depths of my soul, filling the air, replacing our heavy breathing and the sound of my body hitting the wall with sheer shrills of ecstasy.

No warning.

No increased tightening.

No slow climb.

"O-oh, oh!"

It's as if my body forgot how to climax, how to orgasm. I can't focus as the tidal wave of pleasure overcomes me. I'm drowning, rolling in the wave, unsure which direction is up.

My entire body explodes, and I gasp for air. No longer rigid, I puddle in his arms.

"Fuck," he growls as my back continues to pound the wall and my insides spasm uncontrollably around his length.

His deep, possessive roar fills the room as he too comes apart. His thrusts slow, each one less needy, as our breathing settles to a normal rhythm. Once we still, our gazes meet, and both of our smiles widen.

CHAPTER

Eight

Malcolm

I can't believe what we just did.

Okay. We had sex.

Phenomenal, volcanic-erupting, earthshaking, sex. But it felt like so much more.

I hold Mandy tight, like I need to stay inside her, like I can't let her go. The way her arms stay wrapped around my neck and her head rests on my shoulder, I hope she feels the same.

Finally, her legs loosen their grip.

Instantaneously, I miss the warmth of her exposed tits against my chest.

"I don't want to let go of you," I say with my lips against the soft skin of her neck. My voice is a mere whisper as if speaking too loud could break this spell.

"Don't let go." Her voice comes with a sweet giggle as we come apart. As her feet touch the floor, she goes on, "I'm not sure I can walk." With her arms still around my neck, Mandy rises to her tiptoes and gently kisses my cheek. "Thank you."

Why on God's green earth would she be thanking me?

"I'm pretty sure that should be the other way around."

"This is just one night, but you have no idea how special it is...how much I...well, I didn't even know...so, just thank you."

Her words, the way her blue eyes are looking deeply into mine, make me believe she's right. This isn't some casual fuck like those back in my hockey days. Mandy Wells is so much more. "I have a good idea, and thank you."

She just shakes her head as she peers down at the mess I've made of her dress. "Um, maybe I could use your bathroom?"

Quickly pulling my pants back up, I then reach for the buttons on my shirt as I lead her through my apartment. Just before she slips behind the bathroom door, I stop her and shimmy out of the sleeves. "Here," I say, handing her my shirt. "Sorry about your dress."

A flood of pink fills her cheeks as she accepts. "It will clean."

"Your panties..."

Her head tilts. "Yep. I think those are goners." Her eyes sparkle as she closes the door. I hope that the gleam sparkling from her gaze was her way of telling me that her panties were an easy sacrifice for what just happened, for what we just shared.

While she's occupied, I go to the other bathroom and discard the condom. It's been so long since I've needed one that I'm just glad I had it with me. And then I consider the possibility that the night isn't over. I rush to my bedroom, hoping my Boy Scout days paid off and I'm prepared if the opportunity, or anything else, arises.

Over an hour later as I hand Mandy a glass of moscato and her gaze meets with mine, I know undoubtedly that I want to learn everything there is to know about this lady. I don't want us to be strangers, but lovers, friends, soulmates, and everything in between.

In the short time since I've met her, I sense something different than I've experienced in other women. There is honesty and sincerity and an unmistakable loving spark that's hungry for desire and filled with passion. I know it's too soon for me to feel this way, but fuck, I can't help the way I feel.

My smile grows as I take her in, from her beautiful tousled hair to her painted toes. I love the way my green button-down hangs on her, big and gaping, showing just a little of her luscious tits. I can't see all of them, but the curves of the round globes are the perfect tease, making me want more.

"I should probably go," she says, sipping her wine and tugging the hem of my shirt over her knees.

"No."

Her eyes widen. "No? Are you holding me captive?"

My cock comes back to life. "I wasn't thinking that, but now I'm intrigued."

Her smile warms my heart—so trusting and serene.

"But we made a deal before we came here," I remind her.

"We did?"

"I said that before the night was through I wanted to learn more about you, your secrets and dreams. You promised to tell me about the guy you were supposed to meet tonight."

Her cheeks blossom with shades of pink. "It may make me seem awful, but I'm glad I met you instead."

I shake my head, opening my beer. "Not awful at all. You, Mandy Wells, are the best meeting I've had in—well, ever."

She tugs again at the hem of my shirt as her bare legs bend under her sexy, petite body. I love that she's half-naked on my couch. I love that her pussy isn't covered with anything, and I could easily...

She sits straighter. "You're right. We did have a deal, Malcolm, and I believe it included pizza."

My hands go up in the air. "I forgot. You see, I'm quite satis-fied with what I've already eaten."

The pink of her cheeks darkens to a shade of rose as we both entertain memories of the last hour, of her on this same couch, her legs spread wide, and my face buried in her silky cunt as her undecipherable words filled the air. The mere thought of the scene has me ready for a second course.

"Pizza," she says, focusing our thoughts.

I stand and reach for my phone. Before I can pull up the app, I see another text message from Brian. I'd received two earlier at the bar, but with my phone on silent and this gorgeous woman at my side, I hadn't seen them until I was in the car. Truth is that I don't care anymore about the nice woman he wants me to meet. My mind is on Mandy.

I read his text:

Sorry, man, about the mix-up. Sally is going to try to reschedule. I really fucked up. It won't happen next time.

I shake my head, wondering how to respond.

*No worries. The night wasn't a bust. We'll talk. Forget the reschedule, though. I don't think I'm ready for a blind date...*because I want to see the beautiful woman on my couch again, not some "nice" friend of Sally's. I don't text that last part, but I think it.

I look down at Mandy, seeing her eyes on me. The way she's scanning my bare chest makes me want to rip that shirt from her tiny frame. "Well, I never back down from an obligation either," I say. "I promised pizza. What do you like on your pizza?"

Her lips twitch. "Anchovies and jalapeño peppers."

My fingers stop as I pull up the ordering app. "Seriously? Fish?"

Mandy stands, my shirt falling to mid-thigh and walks closer. With each step her breathing appears to take more energy as her chest labors and her eyes widen. "If I said I was serious, that I wanted anchovies and peppers, would you order that?"

It's my turn to nod. Hell, I'd do whatever this woman asked. Make her come all night long. *Yes, ma'am.* Jump from my balcony. *If you say so.*

She shakes her head. "I'm not serious. I'm a veggie girl, but..." Her eyes shimmer and lip disappears for a moment as she looks to my belt and back to my gaze. "...I'm not against meat."

A few clicks and we have a cheese and veggie pizza on its way. By the way she's dropped to her knees and reached for my belt, I'm confident she'll have more than enough meat.

CHAPTER
Nine

Mandy

One night.

That's all this will be.

Dropping to my knees in front of Malcolm, I tell myself to keep going—make it count.

No matter what tomorrow brings, I know that I don't want this amazing feeling to end. I don't want to forget how good it feels to have Malcolm inside me, to have his cock and tongue buried deeply. I want to remember how his hands feel roaming my curves. I don't want to forget the way he makes my entire body ignite and combust.

And perhaps a little selfishly, I also don't want him to forget me.

Reaching for his belt, I allow the tips of my fingers to graze over his lower stomach and trace the indented V at his hips. His hard abs quiver under my touch. I move my fingers lower, closer to his impressive penis as I tease the edge of his pants. My tongue darts to my suddenly dry lips as I unbuckle the belt. My pulse races as I reach for the zipper and unzip his trousers.

It hasn't been that long since he went down on me on the couch, followed by a less urgent fucking. My core is tender and satisfied, yet as my tongue tries unsuccessfully to wet my parched lips, and I caress his velvety length, my satisfaction is waning. I want Malcolm in ways I've never before known. My gaze moves upward through veiled lashes until our eyes meet.

"Mandy, you don't—"

I don't let him finish as I sheath my teeth and take him between my lips.

"Fuck!" His recurring growl sends tremors to my insides as I familiarize myself with his cock. Lifting my body higher, I concentrate on sucking him, taking him deeper into my mouth until he reaches the back of my throat. He smells like us, and despite the use of protection during sex, I taste the scent of us too, like the perfect combination of salt and musk.

It's been so long since I've done this. I fight the urge to gag. It's not that there is anything gag-worthy about Malcolm's cock in my mouth. It's the exact opposite. With each swirl of my tongue and bob of my head, his skin tightens. The cum I missed the first time I fisted him leaks from his tip, and I greedily lap it with my tongue.

He doesn't push me, being so patient, allowing me to work him at my own speed. As I keep going, his balls tighten, pulling closer to his body, and his cock twitches.

"M-Mandy..." My name comes out breathy as I continue moving up and down.

I add my hands to his cock so I'm able to service all of him at once. Though I don't know how it is possible, as I suck and stroke he grows harder than before. Faster and faster I bob my head, fascinated that I'm able to make this incredibly strong man tremble at my touch.

Rolling his balls between my fingertips, my tongue continues to swirl around his tip and lap his length. Tighter and tighter his balls contract as I relish the power.

His breathing is quickening when all of a sudden he pulls away. The apartment, which I finally noticed is a very nice place, echoes with a *pop* as he pulls out of my mouth.

On my knees, I look up, wondering what happened.

"Turn around."

His deep, commanding voice rumbles through me. Only

momentarily confused, I do as he says. Malcolm reaches for my behind and pulls it higher.

"On all fours, beautiful. I'm taking you from behind. You're too sexy—I can't resist."

My ass wiggles with anticipation as I move to the position he demands. Up on my hands and knees, I spread my legs farther apart.

"Look at you," he says.

"I can't..."

My words trail away as he describes what he sees. Though it should embarrass me, it doesn't. The appreciation in his deep tone increases my wanton need.

"So fucking beautiful. Your pussy is pink and wet." His fingers dip inside me, sending shock waves across my skin and leaving goose bumps in their wake. I'm a bundle of nerves, ultrasensitive to his touch. Slowly and deliberately, he spreads my essence until he traces my tight ring of muscles.

My head slowly shakes back and forth as my body tries to make sense of the stimulation. "I-I've never."

Suddenly, his finger pushes through the barrier, going where no one has ever gone. It's erotic and forbidden. The foreign touch is nothing like I expected. Instead of pulling away, I back toward him, little by little taking more and more.

As his finger finds a rhythm, his other hand rubs my clit. The two sensations are all-consuming. Just as the pleasure grows, his cock dives deep inside me. It's overwhelming, skin on skin. It's the most amazing sense of fullness I never knew existed.

"Jesus, that feels...it feels..."

"You feel fucking perfect," he says, finishing my sentence.

Neither one of us mentions the missing protection. It feels too good to stop, to think, to reason. This time the build is slower, but more intense. His finger in my behind was a spark of lightning. Each movement ignites a new wildfire within me. Rubbing my clit is another streak of lightning. My body is alive with a storm of sensations. Flicker by flicker, the energy continues to grow, the heat and intensity continuing to rise until I'm on the brink of a devastating explosion. The storm is now a volcanic eruption ever growing, consuming me as his cock thrusts and his fingers delve and twist.

I willingly rock to his beat, pushing toward his invasion, wobbling on my knees as he pounds into me. It's like nothing I've ever done, nothing I've ever experienced. Annihilation is within sight and I want to experience every molecule-blasting second.

It's out of character.

We're no longer civilized people. Together, in this moment, we are animals, primitive and raw. The pressure, friction, emotion —it all continues to climb. Malcolm's apartment fills with words that neither of us comprehend. Primal noises replace words. Our deep breaths infiltrate our speech as we both struggle to inhale. Perspiration coats our skin. I'm barely aware of the scrape of his teeth as he nips at my shoulder and neck, causing my entire body to tense.

After all we've done tonight, I wonder how I could possibly come again.

I don't know, but all at once the dam breaks, and we both surrender to the inevitable.

Malcolm collapses on top of me as my knees give out. His heart beats erratically against my back as he engulfs me in his embrace. Pulling out and leaving me feeling empty, he rolls me to my back and stares down into my eyes.

The intensity of his gaze mirrors my emotions as a dense cloud of sex lingers in the air. I'm drowning, and yet I don't care. I'm exactly where I want to be.

"Mandy."

I'm mesmerized by the rumble of his voice—not the just the masculine tone, but the way I feel it vibrate from him to me.

"I meant what I said," he continues, "I don't want to let you go. I want more than one night with you."

CHAPTER

Amanda

*I*n his pajamas, Jase runs around the living room of our apartment at the speed of light, his Superman cape cloaking his tiny shoulders. I pull my phone closer to hear my best friend and listen to Sally's apology for the fifteenth time. Shaking my head, I smile at my son's imagination, certain that soon he will have saved the entire planet.

My mom brought him home this morning on her way to the grocery store. And even though she eyed me suspiciously up and down and asked what time I got home, I didn't spill.

I didn't tell her that I didn't come home until the sun was rising or that I'd awakened in Malcolm's bed with his arm draped over my waist. I didn't say that I am completely battered and bruised in the most delicious way. I didn't say that my core and legs are tender or that I'm completely satiated. Instead, I told her the basic truth: I never met up with Sally because Brian had an emergency at work, and I didn't meet my blind date.

Of course, that left out a great number of the facts, but it wasn't a lie.

"He was probably there," Sally says.

"Well, since I'm not sure what he looks like, and he doesn't know me, I don't know."

"Please, Amanda. You have to give it another try," Sally pleads. "You know I would never have left you hanging if it weren't out of my control. Brian feels awful."

"Sally, stop. I don't want you to feel bad. The thing is, I'm not sure I'm ready. I tried. I really did—"

"I know you did. That's why I feel so bad. Just one more time. We'll make sure nothing gets in the way."

"It's just...that was the one night. I don't want to meet Brian's friend. Anyway, I think I should concentrate on Jase and work and let fate work out the rest."

As the words move from my lips through the phone to her ears, I close my eyes.

Fate.

One night.

That's what Malcolm was. Not a blind date, not an arranged meeting, but fate. Fate set up our meeting for one night, and as my skins flushes with memories, I ask myself, who am I to argue with fate?

Sally is still talking. I'm not sure what she is saying, but I assume it is her apology rephrased in essentially the same way, or perhaps she's restating her argument against my stance.

"...can't live like a nun for the rest of your life. You're too young."

"Mom, look at me!" Jase proclaims as he bounces on the couch before jumping to the floor. "I'm flying!"

"You are!"

My son runs toward me, barreling into my lap. His sweet gaze looks up to me. "And I'm fast!"

"And loud," I say with a giggle. "I'm talking to your aunt Sally."

"Hi, Aunt Sally!" Jase yells as he wiggles free and rushes toward his bedroom.

"Besides," I say to the phone, "I have Superman here. I don't think I need any other men, not with Superman."

"Yeah, yeah. Don't make me call your mom."

I almost say that she wouldn't dare, but we both know she would. "The thing is..." I lower my voice. "...I met someone last night. The night wasn't a bust. I'm not sure I'll ever see him again, but it was..." I search for the right word. "...fun."

"What? You what? Holy shit!"

I momentarily pull the phone away from my ear to save my eardrum from splintering as each phrase grows louder.

She continues, "You met someone—like met a *man*? You let me ramble on for hours and apologize a zillion times and you were holding out on me?"

I shake my head playfully. "You were only apologizing and rambling for minutes, not hours. And I'm holding out on everyone. It was only one night. Now you, Mom, Alec, and everyone else can let me be. Besides, he was...nice." I smile at his description of nice. "And for the record, that doesn't mean uglier than shit. I mean nice. He was funny and confident and complimentary—"

"Oh my God! You met someone. How well did you meet him? Did you sleep with him?"

"Remember me? I'm a nun."

"Amanda Jane Wells, spill or I'm coming over."

I shrug. "There's really nothing to spill. Like I said, it was one night. I'd promised you and Mom that I'd remember what it was like to be a woman for one night. I did. End of story."

"Wait! No. Do *not* end the story. I can hear something in your voice. I don't know if you slept with him, but you..." She pauses. "...you did something that made you remember what it's like to be a woman, and I don't think that was buying shoes. There's something. I can hear it!" Her last phrase is so loud that I move the phone away from my ear again.

"It doesn't matter," I say. "I told him it was just one night."

"What? Why?"

Jase runs into the living room, right up to my chair, clutching a jar of peanut butter to his chest. His little eyes flutter as he falls with an agonizing groan to the floor. If he were allergic to peanuts, I might be concerned, but fortunately, he isn't.

"Oh my goodness," I say. "What's the matter, Superman?"

"It's my krip-o-night...I'm dying..."

I smirk, thinking he has the whole kryptonite thing wrong. "Sally, I need to go. Superman is dying."

"I need answers."

"I think he's hungry. I'm pretty sure I can save him. If I don't, I'll let you know."

"A-man-da." She elongates my name.

"Nothing more to tell. Bye. Love you."

After I end the call, I wrangle the jar of peanut butter from Jase's tiny hands and kiss his nose. He's so cute with his eyes closed. It's a moment of peace before he returns to full speed and I do my best to relish the stillness.

Within seconds, he's dashing around the kitchen as I make his lunch. The table is now some kind of cave and from between the legs of the chairs, he's assessing his surroundings before once again stamping out villains.

"Mom?" he asks after he crawls out from his cave and stands beside me.

I look down into his big blue eyes, just like his daddy's. My heart skips a beat as I do a double take.

How hadn't I realized?

Malcolm's eyes are similar to Jase's, a deeper blue than mine. The recognition hurts my chest. Was that why I was attracted to him? He doesn't really look like my husband. Jackson had sandy blond hair like Jase's. Malcolm's hair is dark, closer to mine. Yet it was his eyes, the way they stared at me—really looked at me— that made my tummy do flip-flops. The way they seemed to look not only at me, but also see into my soul. As if he could see more than the surface, like he wanted to see more. But there was also the way he complimented my surface appearance that made me feel beautiful and appreciated in a way I hadn't for so long.

The thoughts cause a lump to form in my throat as I fight to breathe.

"Mommy?" Jase tugs on my shirt.

My hand is on the peanut butter lid, but I haven't moved.

"What, baby?"

"I'm not a baby," he answers matter-of-factly.

"No, you're not." I bend down and poke his tummy. "But you'll always be my baby."

"Even when I'm old?"

"Yep," I confirm with a kiss to his nose. "Now, let me keep making your lunch."

"What if I don't like lunch at my new school?"

I look down, taking in my growing boy. My heart hurts at the thought of him entering school. Sure, he's been in preschool, but this is real school. It's the beginning of growing up, growing older, and moving away. Swallowing back my emotion, I plaster a smile on my face and blink away the moisture. "What makes you think you won't like it? You like lunch at ABC."

His little nose scrunches. "Not always."

"Well, I'll tell you what. If you don't like some of the lunches, I'll pack your lunch on those days."

His eyes widen as if I'm the best mom in the world. If only he would never change his mind. "Really?"

"Yep. I'm pretty sure that we can check the website the week before, and we'll know what they're serving. If there's a day you don't want to eat what they are going to have, I'll make you a sandwich."

"And apple slices?"

"And apple slices."

"Can I get a lunchbox?"

"Of course."

His little arms wrap around my legs. "I love you, Mommy. You're the best!"

My fingers tousle his sandy blond curls. "I love you more."

As I carry Jase's plate to the table, I hear my phone ping. Shaking my head, I say, "Your aunt Sally needs to drop it."

"Drop what? Will she break it?" Jase asks as he scoots into his chair.

"Never mind."

He dives into his sandwich, apple slices, and glass of milk as I reach for my phone.

Malcolm is on the screen.

My heart beats faster.

How? How could his name be in my phone?

I swipe the screen and read the text.

I hope you don't mind, but I sent myself a text from your phone while you were sleeping. This way we each have the other's number. BTW, you have the cutest snore when you're asleep.

My palms moisten. No. This isn't supposed to happen.

I keep reading.

We left this thing with us open. I know you said one night, but without sounding desperate, I meant what I said. I want more.

My eyes close as I try to push away memories of last night, of how great it was, how great he was, his eyes, his smile, his hands...

Now that you know you have my number, I'm waiting for your call or text. Until then, sweet, incredibly sexy Mandy, I'll be busy anticipating your response.

I shake my head.

Shit! Now what do I do?

CHAPTER
Eleven

Malcolm

"You never did tell me what the issue was with the guy you were supposed to meet," I say into my phone, my feet up on my coffee table as I listen to Mandy's soft giggle.

I didn't think she'd call. I was beginning to believe she wouldn't. She'd said she wanted to have only one night. It was starting to look as if that was all it would be.

Yet I didn't give up: I waited and hoped. I can't recall a time—ever—when I've been the one waiting for a phone call, yet I did. Sending myself a text and then sending one to her is not my MO. Then again, everything about her and being with her is different. Mandy's different than the women in my past. She deserves to know how much I enjoyed our one night.

She didn't return my call all day Saturday.

I'd kept my phone with me for the entire day, even refusing to answer the hundred calls from Brian after the one where I told him it was all right, I wasn't upset, and that I didn't want to go out with Sally's friend. I explained how I needed to concentrate on work, especially this time of year. After all, that's what brought me to this city.

"I'm embarrassed to say it," she says softly, regarding my question about her blind-date's issues.

"My curiosity is going wild."

"Well, my friend and her boyfriend think he's been off the dating scene because he can't..." She giggles again and her voice grows softer. "...because he can't get it up."

My cheeks rise as my expression surely mimics some stupid teenager's. "Then I would guess that you went home with the right guy."

"Well, yeah. You didn't seem to have a problem with that...either time."

"Either?" I ask. "Beautiful, I think it was more like five times and no, it wasn't a problem. It wouldn't be a problem now either."

"I-I...this is what I can't do. I'm sorry."

"Don't be sorry. Just talk. I can get it up just at the sound of your voice."

"Oh my!"

"That's it. Now if you'd moan or whimper in that cute way you do—"

"Malcolm, stop," she says in a hushed tone. "I can't have phone sex with you while my son is asleep in the other room."

Fuck. I'd forgotten all about her son. It's not that I care if she has a kid. I love kids. If I didn't, I wouldn't have chosen my new profession. I wouldn't have gone back to school and gotten my degree or moved to this city, seizing the chance to do something meaningful. "Sorry. I forgot."

Mandy goes quiet on the other end.

"Don't stop talking. I was just imagining that pink blush on your cheeks. I'm not really getting off, not yet anyway."

A long sigh fills the silence, coming from her end. "The other night...I-I had a good time..."

My cheeks rise. "I had a better-than-good time. It has been a long time since I've had such an amazingly good time. I'm not sure I ever have. I understand you have responsibilities. I get that. I'll take whatever time you can spare."

"How?"

"How?" I repeat her question. "What do you mean?"

"Don't you work?"

"I do. This is Sunday night. I work during the week, normal hours. You?"

"Same."

"And your son goes to bed..." I let my sentence go unfinished.

"Tonight is early. He starts school Tuesday, and I've been trying to get him in a good routine. But as I said, I don't plan to introduce you. It's not fair to him."

I nod my head, liking that she's protective. That's the way moms should be. "As much as I want to come to your house and come at your house...and make you come at your house—"

"Malcolm!"

"Right, as I was saying...I get it. I respect it. Can we perhaps plan another date? A real one. Dinner and drinks. Not pizza and rehydration."

"I don't know. I think I liked pizza and rehydration."

"Fuck, now you're the one with the sexy tone."

Mandy giggles again, and I imagine her cheeks a stunning shade of crimson.

"I need to check with my mom. She and my dad will probably watch him. They're great."

"When does he go to his father's house?"

She doesn't respond. As the silence grows, I get the sickening feeling that I've overstepped my bounds. "Mandy, I'm sorry. That is none of my business. Please, talk to your parents. My friend is determined to get me to meet that *nice* lady, but I told him that I'm seeing someone."

"No! Malcolm, we met. It was one night. We aren't *seeing* one another."

"Oh, sexy. I've seen you—all of you—and I want to see all of you again and again. And now you've called me back. That must mean something. You also left my place Saturday. So technically, it was one night and a morning. That makes two days."

"No promises," Mandy says with a sigh. "My friend is after me too. But I've told her a thousand times that I don't want to see anyone. I guess maybe I should start to rephrase that. I don't want to see anyone—"

Her tone lingers...as if she has more to say. I sit up, plant my feet on the floor, and grasp the phone tighter. "Anyone...?" I encourage. "...go on."

"Anyone except you."

Yes!

"Now that's what I'm talking about. A date, Ms. Wells, a real date. You name the day and time, and I'll be the gentleman I wasn't Friday night."

Her voice stays low. "I'm admittedly out of practice, but you seemed rather gentlemanly to me. You opened my car door at the restaurant, at your place, and again when I needed to leave. You gallantly offered me your shirt when my dress became...compromised."

My cheeks rise higher. "I'll go along with the car door, but the shirt was purely for my benefit."

"Yours?"

"Do you have any idea how sexy you looked wearing it?"

"And to think, I'd worked hard to buy the perfect dress. I guess my time was wasted."

I love the lighthearted glee that's back in her tone. "No, not wasted. I guess the poor sap with erection issues didn't get to appreciate it, but I certainly did. You were stunning—in and out of that dress. However, without you in it, it's just a piece of material."

"I'm sitting in my living room barefoot, in old shorts and a T-shirt, and yet somehow you're making me feel pretty."

"You should never doubt that. Ever."

"It's nice to hear. Thank you."

"I want to learn more about you than your looks. From the moment you sat on the stool beside me, I was attracted to you." When she doesn't speak, I go on, "Everything about you...one of the first things that caught my attention is your gorgeous hair. It's rich and full. I like how it flows over your shoulders. If I close my eyes, I can see you in that booth, and I remember how badly I wanted to reach out and run my fingers through it."

"Well, now, it's twisted into a messy knot."

I lean back, imagining her hair on the pillow beside me. "Not to devalue your hard work in preparation for Mr. Issues, but honestly, as lovely as it was at the restaurant, I think it was the most beautiful on my pillow, fanning out like a halo around your face."

"Malcolm..."

The way she says my name sounds breathy, and I wish with everything in me that I could go to her. "Fuck. You said no phone sex, right?"

"Right," Mandy agrees, though her tone sounds like she might consider changing her mind.

"Then, instead of my remembering how fantastic you were the other night, how stunning and perfect...let's concentrate on our upcoming date."

"I-I don't..."

"Whenever you want. I'll wait. I'm not rushing you. You arrange for your son to be taken care of and let me handle everything else. Okay?"

The silence goes on and on. My pulse increases as the TV silently plays some pre-season NHL footage. For the first time that I can ever remember, I don't care about what's on the screen. My concern isn't about the stats or the prognosticators, but about the lady on the other end of this call. With each second, I grow more concerned that she'll change her mind about going out with me again. I'm almost tempted to speak, to say anything that may help my case and sway her decision my way, but before I do, she finally answers.

"Okay."

I let out the breath I was holding. "Can I call you tomorrow night?"

"After eight-thirty."
"My new favorite time of the day."
"Bye, Malcolm."
"Bye, beautiful Mandy."

CHAPTER
Twelve

Amanda

Beautiful Mandy. The phrase runs on a loop through my mind as I lie in my darkened bedroom and try to drift off to sleep.

Like every night before coming to bed, I checked on Jase. Tonight, I spent a few extra minutes marveling at my son, watching his small body, and covering him with his blanket as he dreamt about whatever it is he dreams. It hurts sometimes at how much I love him, how much I want to keep him safe and secure. There's a mother bear inside me that loves when he's in his bed hibernating because I know it's a haven. I know he's safe. Yet I can't keep him there. I have to let him live and spread his wings. No matter how hard I wish otherwise, Jase is growing up, and I can't make it stop. It's hard to believe that tomorrow is his last day at ABC Preschool.

How has time moved this fast? It seems like yesterday when he was born, when Jackson was holding his pink and wrinkled little body.

But it wasn't yesterday. So much has changed since Jackson and I brought him home to his new little nursery. Even where Jase and I live has changed. I don't regret moving closer to my parents. Things have been as good as they could be, but Tuesday will be another change and admittedly, it frightens me.

Kindergarten shouldn't scare me as much as it does. I mean, it's all about shapes and letters and colors. It's learning to share and how to use a cubby. It is many things he already knows from preschool, my parents, and me. Jase is smart, downright brilliant if you ask me. This transition shouldn't be scary. And even though I feel like it is, I've done my best not to relay that fear to my son. Yet the reality is that beginning kindergarten is going to be new and different, and I'm not a fan of change. Not a fan of different. Not a fan of surprises.

It's never for the better.

My chest aches with the thought of sending him to the big school with all the new classmates. I say a silent plea that he makes friends. Sally and I became friends when we were a little older, but Alec and Jackson were in the same kindergarten class. Maybe Jase could make lifelong friends. I think of Alec. He's not usually as sensitive as he was the other night, and I never doubted his love for my husband. What would my brother think about the man fate brought to me?

Beautiful Mandy.

I know Jase needs to be allowed to live. Do I?

Would Jackson really want me to agree to see Malcolm again, or would he think I should go back to the way I've been? I try to think of how I'd feel if our roles were reversed—if I were gone, if Jackson were raising Jase.

My thoughts go to Malcolm.

Beautiful Mandy.

A smile comes to my lips.

Malcolm is something different, something new. What I did with him, what we did together, was out of character. Totally. Just like Alec told me to be. But it wasn't meant to be a springboard to a new relationship. It was meant to be my one night to remember that I'm more than a mom, daughter, sister, friend, and employee —that I'm a woman.

The last time I had sex—before the mini-marathon Friday night—was before Jase was born. Immediately following Jase's birth, I couldn't. Jackson didn't mind. He understood. Jackson always understood. Besides, he was due to return home in three months. We both believed there would be time.

Now, I wonder what I'm doing with my time.

Even if I'd never returned Malcolm's call, during our one night he gave me exactly what I'd been seeking: the reminder that I am a sensuous woman. He gave me that multiple times.

I struggled with whether or not to call him back after I received his text message. There were so many times on Saturday when I reached for my phone, only to put it back down. On Saturday, I let my principles win. I stuck to my guns and senses. I kept telling myself that I didn't want a relationship. I don't need that complication in my life. Most importantly, Jase doesn't need it.

That worked until I had trouble remembering my reasons for not calling. Until I remembered how special I felt with him.

Tonight, I caved.

Beautiful Mandy.

Special, pretty, and even treasured.

Tonight, while we were on the phone, his deep voice filled me with a sense of being something special—something more than just a tired mom. It's not like I have self-esteem issues. I don't. And I'd like to think I wouldn't be described as *nice*—as in uglier than shit. The thought makes me smile as I imagine Malcolm describing his blind date.

While I don't have issues with low self-esteem, I also don't have anyone to boost my self-confidence. I have Jase, who tells me I'm pretty. But we all know that will change when Alec teaches him about ponytails and dimples. Once my son discovers girls, his mom won't be the prettiest woman anymore. I also have my parents. They are always complimentary. And there's Alec who teases me about my breasts, or lack thereof. Yet none of those people's praise or ribbing makes me tingle the way I do when Malcolm calls me beautiful.

As I think back on Friday night, he'd even said that to the bartender, told him I was beautiful and gorgeous, before we ever spoke.

Staring up at the dark ceiling, looking for justification, I know that I called Malcolm tonight because I stopped thinking about why I shouldn't call and began considering why I wanted to. I recalled how within minutes of meeting, Malcolm calmed my trepidation at being alone in the bar. I remembered the ease of our conversation and the warmth of his skin as he fell asleep holding me tightly to his frame. I recalled the security of sleeping in his arms and what it felt like to not be alone.

Before I called, I tried to tell myself that I was acting crazy. I barely know the man. And while it's quite obvious he doesn't have an erection issue, that doesn't mean he doesn't have other issues.

And now that I have called, I keep wondering.

He said he is employed. But what don't I know? While my brain says his issues could be something serious like a police record, tremendous debt, or a family history of mental-health problems, my heart tells me to stop exaggerating. If Malcolm Peppernick has issues, it's probably something more like he stays up too late, likes scary movies, or worse, doesn't sleep in on the weekends.

My pulse kicks up a notch.

I love to sleep in, any chance I get. I could never be with a man who's an early riser.

What if he is a runner? Or long-distance bicyclist?

Staring at the ceiling, I imagine the horror of dating a man who enjoys exercise. I don't think I can do that. What if he'd want me to exercise too?

My heart beats faster.

What if he doesn't like chocolate or doesn't drink coffee?

I sit up in my dark bedroom and wonder why I called him back. Why did I agree to another date? This isn't right. I can't bring a non-chocolate-eating, non-coffee-drinking exercise freak into my son's life.

It's all coming back.

This is why I didn't want to meet Brian's friend, the ex-hockey player. Now, instead of lying in bed and worrying about Jase starting kindergarten, my mind is awhirl with Malcolm. As the minutes tick away, I decide it's too much. I have too much on my plate as a working single mom and with my family to complicate life even more with a crazy bicycle-distance-riding, anti-caffeine chocolate hater.

No one needs that in their lives. Not me. Not Jase.

No wonder Malcolm isn't dating anyone. I mean, a man as handsome as Malcolm should have a line of women.

It's probably because all of those other women aren't as rusty on the dating scene as I am. They all saw what I didn't. It's because he won't eat brownies! Who doesn't eat brownies?

Health nuts. That's who.

I throw back the covers and jump from my bed, my mind churning and flooding with a tsunami of unanswered questions. How did I miss it? I didn't see the signs, but I'm sure they were there. We ate pizza. No one even mentioned dessert. What about birthdays? What if he won't eat cake? That just isn't right!

I pace back and forth beside my bed. Outside my bedroom window, beyond the slightly opened shutters, is the parking lot. Friday night I was at Malcolm's apartment and my car was in his parking lot.

Change. Different.

That can't happen again. Not if he's going to put dessert restrictions on my life. Not if he'll want me to exercise. This has to end before it gets out of hand.

Before I can stop myself, I reach for my phone and type a text.

Coffee – for or against? Chocolate – for or against? What about exercise?

I know I shouldn't send it, but I need sleep. If I'm going to save puppies at work tomorrow and get Jase ready for his first day of school, I can't have these monumental issues hanging over my head.

Taking a deep breath, I hit send.

It's after eleven. Normally, I'd be asleep. Yep. This is his fault, too. I can't do it. Once he confesses his odd hatred for all things sweet, we can call it quits, and I can get on with my life. Stop this thing before it goes any further.

With a huff, I settle against my headboard and pull my covers over my bent knees. The light on my phone fades, yet I hold my cell phone tight, staring at the dark screen.

"Oh, don't pretend you're not awake. I know you stay up too late, trying to mess with my schedule, probably planning out your twelve-mile run or making a shopping list for everything gluten-free. If we weren't meant to eat gluten, God wouldn't have made flour!"

Yes, I'm talking aloud to a man who isn't here. I realize it may seem silly, yet this has to end. As soon as he comes clean, it's over.

Just as I'm about to place my phone back on the bedside stand, it pings.

(Smile emoji) Hell yes. Not against it, especially the syrup that goes on ice cream...in the shower or on plastic sheets, it could be fun. And if the exercise includes you and the chocolate syrup, I'm in.

A giant smile breaks out across my face as I stare at his response.

I like chocolate syrup. I've never done what he's suggesting, but then again, I'd never done that other thing that he did either.

My cheeks warm. I guess I can cross coffee, sweets, and gluten hater off my list.

I text back.

Goodnight, Malcolm.

My phone pings.

Goodnight, beautiful Mandy. I wish you were here. But I'll wait.

It's then I realize that I didn't truly settle the gluten issue. And then I recall him eating pizza.

With a sigh, I settle against my pillow. As sleep grows nearer I realize something else: instead of lying here worrying about kindergarten, my mind is saturated with chocolate syrup, and I'm smiling ear-to-ear.

CHAPTER

Mandy

I ease into the booth and smile toward Malcolm's welcoming expression.

"Hello, gorgeous."

Despite any qualms I may have been having, my smile grows as his greeting fills me with a welcomed feeling of warmth. "I'm sorry this is a late dinner. I wanted to wait until...my son was in bed."

Malcolm shakes his head. "Not a problem. I ordered you a glass of moscato. I hope you don't mind."

There's a tug in my chest, remembering how Jackson used to do that—order things for me. Though I have friends who would be offended by a man ordering for them, I'm not one. On the contrary, I'm pleased that Malcolm remembers the type of wine that I like. It's sweet—the wine and him. "I don't mind. Thank you."

Malcolm reaches across the table and opens his hand, palm up.

Slowly I lift mine and place it in his. My eyes flutter as his fingers encase mine. The energy at our connection ripples through me, waking me and bringing my tired body back to life. It's like electricity recharging me after my long day at work, my concerns over Jase's kindergarten class, and life in general. For only a moment, I fantasize how it would be to have Malcolm's warmth and support every evening.

"You're too far away."

My gaze moves back to his blue eyes and his sexy smile. "I am? We're touching."

His brow lifts suggestively. "Not in as many places as I'd like."

"Didn't you promise me dinner and drinks?"

"I did." Just as he speaks, the waitress arrives with glasses of water, a glass of moscato, and another of beer.

Once she's gone, Malcolm verbalizes my thoughts. "After a long day at work, it's nice to sit here and talk, sharing a drink and touching."

I nod, especially liking the last one. "I was thinking the same thing."

"Tell me about your job."

I take a deep breath and let it out. "Can all that wait?"

We've spoken on the phone every night since Sunday. Sometimes it's for a few minutes; other nights it's until way past my normal bedtime. It seems as though all the things I worried about aren't truly concerns. Malcolm likes coffee, all day during the cold months and definitely every morning. Besides chocolate syrup, he does enjoy an occasional cookie, brownie, and has never turned down birthday cake. Like any normal human being, he prefers buttercream frosting to fondant or whipped. Who doesn't? He also enjoys reading, more so than any other man I've known. I've never been able to talk books with anyone except Sally, and I like the discussions Malcolm and I have shared. We both agree that releasing *Go Set a Watchman* was a mistake. He's also addicted to Netflix originals and suggested we go to the movies sometime, though he's tired of remakes and thinks Hollywood needs some new original ideas.

I couldn't agree more.

It's the real-life issues that we've kept to a minimum.

"Wait for what?" he asks.

"I don't really know. I think I want to enjoy being with you without it being too real. My job has its ups and downs. I love the company I work for and my coworkers. My manager can be a real bitch..." The fingers from my other hand fly to my lips. It's one thing to say that to Sally, but I don't know Malcolm well enough to talk that way, and I don't want him to think less of me.

Before I can take it back, his laugh resonates, filling the space of our booth and reverberating through me. "Now don't get all shy on me. I guarantee I heard worse expletives from your lips than that one each time you came apart with me buried deep inside you."

My eyes widen as I giggle at his observation. "I guess...I didn't realize..."

He leans across the table, squeezing my hand and lowering his voice. "You didn't realize you like to yell *fuck* when you're coming apart."

I suck my upper lip between my teeth to squelch my grin and slowly shake my head. "No. I didn't realize."

His blue eyes dance in amusement. "Then I'm quite proud of myself."

"You are?"

"Yes, I had you so distracted you didn't know what you were saying."

My cheeks warm as blood rushes to the surface.

"By the way, you were also confessing your undying love for me."

This time my lips purse. "I think you're exaggerating."

"Maybe a little."

We release one another's hand as we lift our respective glasses.

"To you," Malcolm proposes his toast. "To us, and to avoiding nice women and men with erectile issues."

I nearly spit out my wine as I take a sip.

Though we avoid discussing anything too revealing, the conversation never lags. Like the first night and all the nights on the phone, talking to him is easy and fun. Through our meal and as we sip a cup of coffee to postpone the inevitable goodbye, we laugh, smile, and simply chat. It's refreshing and new, exciting yet comfortable. Our date, the evening as a whole, is everything I've wanted—times a thousand. It's almost eleven when Malcolm pays the bill.

"My place?" he asks.

I shake my head. "I want to." *And I do.* "But my friend is watching Ja—" I stop before I say Jase's name. "My son. If I get back too much later, she'll never stop asking questions."

Malcolm reaches for my hand and our fingers intertwine. "Let me walk you to your car. I promised to be a gentleman. That means there's a door to open."

The night air holds the slight chill of impending autumn as we walk across the nearly empty parking lot. As we approach my car, his grip of my hand tightens, and he lowers his lips to my ear. "Did I mention how stunning you are tonight?"

Instinctively, I turn and brush my lips over his. "You're very handsome, too."

"That dress is lovely, but..." His words trail into the night.

We're now at my car. I'm leaning against it and looking up at him. With only the tall lights of the parking lot, his features are shadowed. His protruding brow is more pronounced, and his shoulders seem wider. What I said is true. Malcolm is handsome, incredibly so.

"But?" I ask, prompting him to go on.

"For the last five days, I've imagined you the way you were, on your knees, fully exposed..." He leans closer. Even in his jeans his erection is prominent. "...and I want to see you that way again."

Maybe it's the coffee we just drank, but I'm pretty sure what I'm feeling is brought on by more than caffeine. His proximity, words, and tone comprise the accelerant making my blood race. My insides tighten in a painful knot of desire, confirming that despite my declining his invitation, I want to go with him. I want more tonight than a good girl's dinner and drinks.

"Malcolm..."

Before I can say more, his lips capture mine and his fingers twist my low ponytail until my head moves backward. All at once his kisses pepper my neck, my exposed skin, sending heat to my chilled flesh. My body's on fire and this sweet, sexy man is the match. It's his spark that ignites the inferno.

"When...?" His voice is gravelly with desire.

I can't think about anything except the raging blaze within me. I'm consumed by his lips, the way they kiss and suck. His teeth, the way they nip and bite. His beard, the way it tickles and prickles. And the part of him that is hard and pressed against my stomach, reminding me what could be.

"When can I see you again...like that?" he asks again.

"I'll try." It's all I can promise, but as my response hangs in the night air, my hand seems to develop a mind of its own, dropping to the front of his jeans and rubbing his erection with all my force. Below my fingers as I move up and down across the coarse denim, he hardens and grows. It's such a primal response, yet as his eyes close and breath stutters, I'm reminded of something I'd forgotten. His reaction reminds me that even with a tall, handsome man like Malcolm, I am a woman with the ability to affect him. It's empowering and makes me want more.

"Fuck." Again, his growl is a whispered rumble.

Or is it a promise?

"I thought you said I was the one who cursed?" I ask.

"I want to hear that too." He lifts my hand to his lips and gently kisses my knuckles. "Mandy, you deserve much better, but may I please have a little more of your time?"

I look around the parking lot. It's true that it's nearly empty, but I can't fathom what he has in mind. "What do you want?"

"Oh, beautiful. I want you."

Five minutes later, with Malcolm in my passenger seat, we park at the far back lot of a neighborhood park not too far from the restaurant. It's rather secluded and probably supposed to be off-limits this time of night. With no streetlights and a ring of trees surrounding the parking area, it's mostly dark; the only exception comes from the stars visible high above the canopy of trees.

I can't believe we're here on public property about to do what we're about to do.

My heart is beating out of control, and my entire body is on alert.

This is dangerous.

This is sexy.

This is stupid.

This is erotic.

This is something that sex-crazed teenagers would do, not grown adults...and then it hits me...

This is something Mandy Wells would do.

Malcolm reaches for the button on his jeans, but before he undoes it, I lean over. "Let me."

The sense of empowerment grows as I unfasten his button and lower his zipper. His mammoth length springs forward. Commando is how he is—nothing beneath his jeans but his giant erection. Embracing the inner vixen I never knew I had, I give Malcom my biggest smile as I lean forward and lick the musky dew from his tip. My actions elicit a deep, reverberating groan from somewhere in his chest. When I look up, his sparkling eyes are on me.

"Beautiful Mandy, there isn't a lot of room in here. Shimmy out of those panties and come sit on my dick."

I giggle as I sit up and reach under my dress for my underwear. "If that's your best pickup line, I now understand why you aren't seeing anyone."

As he sheaths his massive erection, I pull my panties down my legs, shamelessly leaving them on the driver's-side floorboard. With my panties gone, my core clenches in anticipation as I climb from my seat to his. My hands grab ahold of his shoulders as my knees straddle his lap.

"You're wrong," he says.

"I am?" I look around, wondering if he had something else in mind.

"Not about your position, beautiful. You're right where I want you. You're wrong about me."

"About you?"

"I am seeing someone." He scans me up and down. "I'm seeing you." He reaches to the front of my dress and undoes the row of buttons. Like last time, he pushes my bra down until my beaded nipples are peeking over the cups. Palming one of my breasts, he praises me again. "Your tits are perfect. Made for my hands."

My head falls back as I groan and writhe with his caresses, but it's as he shifts and his fingers find my entrance that I let loose my first curse word. All at once, the walls of my pussy clench around his fingers.

"You're always so wet."

I shake my head. "No, not always. Only when I'm with you."

Malcolm lines up the tip of his cock, purposely holding my hips away, teasing and building my anticipation. And then all at once he guides my body, yanking me down, hard and fast, surrounding his rod as my essence allows him to slide into place.

"Oh!" My mouth stays in an 'O' even after the word trails away.

So deep.

In this position his cock is a thick rod, a post, staking his claim. Buried inside me, he makes me squirm as he stretches and fills me. Though I have a sense of control, it's his hands guiding my hips, moving them in time with his.

The friction is staggering as my knees flex, and I ride him up and down.

His lips continue to suck my nipples, pulling, biting, and marking them.

The night's chill disappears as perspiration coats our skin and the windows fog.

"You're so tight. So fucking good." Malcolm's admiration is

stilled only when his lips are busy. The scruff of his beard abrades my sensitive skin in the most erotic way. Despite the heat inside the car, my nipples are rock-hard as he continues to move me, allowing me to ride him. Then he reaches for my clit. The newfound friction is cosmic as flashes of light explode behind my eyes. I'm no longer aware of what I'm saying or the sounds coming from my mouth.

Harder and harder one of his hands grips my hip while the other teases my clit. His hold is so tight that I wonder if I'll have bruises of his fingerprints upon my skin, and then all at once, we both come, our bodies detonating together. We're like fireworks connected to the same fuse, and the epic explosion is a grand finale.

My head falls to his shoulder as I catch my breath. Only the panting of our gasps is audible as we settle into the cloud of his masculine scent and our lovemaking. He holds me tight until our heartbeats begin to slow.

"That was fucking great," he says.

I nod against his neck as a smile tugs at my lips. "It was."

CHAPTER

Fourteen

Malcolm

"Mr. Peppernick, I asked you here today to offer you the position of our middle-school boys' head soccer coach. As you may know, Mr. Ellis, the current head coach, is undergoing medical treatment that makes it difficult, if not impossible, for him to maintain the coaching schedule."

I stare at the school district's athletic director, Mr. Keys, as I consider his offer. "You know I played hockey, right?"

His stoic expression melts. "Yes, we're all aware of that. And since I've been a Blackhawks fan for all of my life, I have more than a few memories of you ruining our hopes at the Stanley Cup."

Scenes from my past flood my thoughts. Like an old play reel, I remember the long days, the hard work, and the longer nights. The hotels and travel. The season, the playoffs, and the adrenaline.

Twice during my career, it was the Lightning Bolts versus the Blackhawks in the playoffs. The year we won the Stanley Cup, the Hawks had the home-ice advantage. We stole that from them in the second game—I stole it—with a last-second shot that sent us into overtime. You'd think after the first overtime our players would have been tired or theirs would have been. No, overtime is like a drug to athletes, the intense unrelenting need to keep playing overrules all else. Our bodies may hurt like hell the next day, but while it's happening, we're on overdrive.

Our goalie was standing on his head, saving us many times. That year, the Blackhawks had some of the top scorers in the league. It was the final seconds of the second overtime when Brian managed to get the puck away from one of the Hawks. It happened so fast that I recall the scene more from the highlight reels than from real life. As the buzzer was about to sound, Brian sent a Hail Mary sailing down the ice. That series never made it to the seventh game. It was the Lightning's only Stanley Cup win.

I smile. "So is coaching middle-school soccer my penance?"

The truth is I went into teaching because of the work I did with kids and hockey. The team's public relations people wanted us to do volunteer work. I'll admit it all began that way. But after I started, I couldn't stop. I loved getting to know the kids at the camps, so much so that I volunteered with the U12 hockey league in Clearwater. It wouldn't seem that in a hot state like Florida there would be that many kids who were interested in hockey, but there are. Maybe it was the ice. Maybe it was the hard work and camaraderie of being part of a team. Maybe it was that watching the Lightning inspired them. Whatever it was, I looked forward to my volunteer work as much as my real work.

I didn't only volunteer my time, but also money. Equipment isn't inexpensive. It didn't seem right to me that some child should be deprived of the chance to play based solely on financial inability. I helped create scholarships that are still in place. I still contribute financially, and with the way the scholarship trust was set up, the money should be available for a long time.

The other players who volunteered with me and I saw lives change. Kids who were lost and aimless became focused. Parents told us stories and the kids even brought their report cards in to us to show us their progress. It was as rewarding as winning the cup to see a kid turn his life around because of skates, a stick, and a puck.

Mr. Keys laughs at my question. "I don't think coaching will be that bad, and hockey and soccer have their similarities."

"They do, but it might take more than shin guards to protect against the blades on the skates and the field may need repair."

"Yeah, you'll have to talk to Julia, the secretary in the athletic department, if you plan on a uniform change."

"Got it. No skates, only cleats?"

"Right. The thing is that the tryouts for this season are done. The team is set. Paul thought he could do it, but with each day it's gotten too difficult for him to keep going. His doctor wants him to concentrate on getting well and so do we. Practices are at the middle-school field every school day at 3:15 unless there's a game. Those are either Tuesday or Thursday after school, or some games are on Saturday mornings. As you know, the middle school is only a five-minute drive from your school. The assistant coach works at the middle school and can get the students started with warm-ups if you have a conflict and know you'll be late."

"And you don't want to offer this position to the assistant coach?" I ask, not wanting to step on toes.

"The assistant coach doesn't have a Stanley Cup ring."

"But I bet the assistant coach knows the students and the game of soccer better than I do."

"The assistant coach is Rita Sanchez, a PE teacher at the middle school. She knows the students. She knows the game. She loves soccer, played all through college. She is also seven months pregnant." His smile grows. "For obvious reasons, she would like to continue as assistant for the time being."

Like many other times during my days, my mind goes to Mandy.

We've only been seeing each other for a little over a month—since fate put us together at the same restaurant bar—but, nevertheless, as I'm contemplating my decision, I think of her. I've been single for so long that it surprises me that I wonder what she'd think of this opportunity.

I realize that as I face different decisions, I'd like to share them with someone—no, not someone, with her. I know my decision won't affect us. Rarely do we see one another before eight-thirty or nine at night and never on Saturday mornings, unless it's very early and a continuation of Friday night. I understand her desire to protect her son, but that doesn't mean I don't wish for more.

However, apparently by the expression of anticipation on Mr. Keys's face, I don't have time to consult with anyone. He wants an answer, and if I want to do this, I need to move.

"I'll be honest," Mr. Keys says, "the additional money isn't that much. It's hardly an NHL position."

"If I say yes, it won't be for the money." And I never wanted a coaching position with the NHL. If I had, I'd have gone a different route with my future. I'm grateful for my years as a hockey player. I wouldn't trade them for anything, but when I left the sport, I did that because I was done with it professionally. Of course, I'm still a fan. I even have season tickets though I'm now five states away.

If I'm willing to give up my afternoons and some Saturday mornings, it's because of the memories I have of kids' hockey camps and teams. Yes, now I see similar excited expressions on the students in my classroom, but to have that same enthusiasm I see there *for* a sport, that is the reason I'll say yes. I want to help the boys on this team learn to love the hard work as much as the fun and excitement of a game.

I nod my head. "In that case, it seems like time is of the essence in making this decision."

"I'm sorry that I can't give you more time to think about it, but we're between a rock and a hard place. The games begin soon and we need an official coach."

"I'd be honored to be the coach."

Mr. Keys's smile blooms, filling his face as he extends his hand and we shake. "I couldn't be happier, Malcolm, and for the record, I really did hate you when you played." He shakes his head. "Not so much *you*, because if you'd played for the Blackhawks, I would have been your biggest fan. We're honored to have you here teaching in our district."

"The honor is mine."

"Someday, I'd love to hear the story of your turn with the cup."

I just laugh as I answer, "Another day. When do I start coaching?"

"Rita would like to introduce you to the kids now, this afternoon, if you can stop by the field. Then talk to her and she'll fill you in on the rest of the schedule."

As I drive toward the middle school, I can't help but think that I wish I could tell Mandy about this tonight during our call. Despite the comment about penance, I am excited, and I want to share that with her. I know she doesn't want to get too personal, but whether she admits it or not, from the first night we met it's been personal.

CHAPTER
Fifteen

Amanda

We all clap our approval. I'm not sure if it's because my brother's softball game is over or because he won. Jase bounces up and down as he screams his uncle's name. Despite the din of the people, Alec turns toward us and waves. I like when my brother's games are on non-school nights and earlier in the evening. I don't know whose bright idea it was to schedule men's softball at ten-thirty at night, but that is definitely not conducive to the attendance of three-foot-tall fans.

As the crowd begins to move from the bleachers and the next two teams take the field, I start to get up, but before I do, my dad stops me.

"How about Jase and I head over to the concession stand?"

Jase's eyes widen in a silent plea as he waits for my answer.

I reach for my wallet. "You don't have to buy—"

Dad interrupts me. "Give this old man a break. Your mom isn't here, and I can buy my grandson ice cream." He winks. "The kid is my cover story."

My dad loves ice cream.

I can't help but laugh. The truth is that he'd go to the concession stand even if Mom were here. "Sure. I'll wait here."

"Good plan. Plausible deniability."

"What ice cream?" I ask.

Dad takes Jase by the hand, and together, they head down the bleachers.

Though it's just past dusk, with the lights over the fields, the sky looks black. Taking this opportunity to enjoy a moment of peace, I peer up at the sky. As I do, my mind goes back to Malcolm's and my visit to a different city park on the other side of town. My cheeks flush as I think about what would have happened if we'd been caught.

Bringing my gaze back to this ballfield, I see men of all ages. Many have been my parents' friends, as well as parents and siblings of my and Alec's friends. They are people I've known most of my life, and I know for certain that some of the guys on Alec's team are part of the local police force.

I think of what could have happened if Malcolm and I had been caught. I would have officially died from embarrassment if one of these men or women would have found us parked back in that isolated lot. Despite what is supposed to happen when the police find someone in that situation, I'm certain that if that had happened, if one of my brother's friends would have come upon my car, there would have been no confidentiality, no professional courtesy. Whoever found us probably would have called Alec while I was sitting right there. I can imagine one of them now: *Hey Alec, I'm holding your sister and some man in my patrol car with a pending charge of indecent exposure. Do you want to come pick her up, or should I call your folks?*

Honestly, it would be more embarrassing now than if it'd happened ten years ago.

"How's kindergarten going?" Alec asks as he plops down next to me on the aluminum bleacher, his body weight and large equipment bag landing with a thud and making me jump.

"I'd rather not think about it. Jase is having fun tonight. Let's let him be?"

"Okay. Then tell me about your date."

"There was no blind date." I've gotten good at sticking to that story.

"Yeah, I heard. Mom said that something came up with Brian and you never met up with his friend? Is Brian's patient okay?"

"Yeah, I think everything worked out. Mostly Sally has apologized. Like I said, the blind date was a bust."

He nudges my shoulder with his.

I flinch away from his moist touch. His shirt is saturated with an aromatic combination of perspiration, dirt, and grime from his recent game. "Bro!" I scrunch my nose. "You stink."

Alec laughs. "Fine. I smell, but you stink at lying."

He nudges me again as I make 'ew' sounds and dramatically scoot away. We may be adults, but there's part of me that wants to yell to my father, "Dad, Alec's touching me. Make him stop touching me." Then I remember that I'm a parent and I can't do that.

"Look at you," Alec says with a sly, lopsided grin.

"What?"

"Tell big brother all about this guy. I'm not out of the loop. I know you've gone on a few dates. I want to help. I mean..." He nods to his friend Steve Stivey who actually caught two long fly balls in left field tonight, sitting with his wife a few rows down. "...give me a name and date of birth, and Steve can run a nice detailed report. In minutes, we'll know everything: parking tickets, moving violations, misdemeanors, felonies..."

I shake my head. "You know why I love living in a small town connected to other small towns where it seems like everyone knows everyone?"

"Because we all have your back?"

"No. I was being sarcastic. It was a rhetorical question."

Alec pulls out his phone. "Give me your phone. I can start with his contact information."

I lean back and tuck my phone tightly into my lap. "No."

"Listen, I know I said it was a good idea to go on that date, but now, this is different. You know what they say...better safe than sorry. I owe it to Jackson and Jase."

"First, what I told Mom was accurate. Brian had some work-related emergency. He and Sally didn't make it, so if the other guy, Brian's friend, was there, I never met him."

"The *other* guy...implies that there's *another* guy."

I start to stand, but before I can, Alec reaches for my hand. "I'm really not being an ass."

"You are. Have I ever offered to do background checks on every woman you sleep with?"

Alec's cocky smile evaporates before me as his blue eyes darken and forehead furrows. "You slept with him?"

"Oh! Shit. This conversation isn't happening."

"Listen," he says in a hushed tone. "It was one thing when it was Brian's friend. Brian's an all-right guy. He's even subbed on the team a few times and comes to Wayne's Place with Sally sometimes. It was one thing when you were going to meet *his* friend. This is a pickup."

"When did you get so critical? It wasn't a pickup. It was fate, and it was one night. So you don't need to worry about Jase. Like I said the other night, I'm not telling him."

"But you've gone out with this other guy a few more times?"

"So?"

"So that's more than one night. Stivey can run a quick—"

I lean down and kiss my brother's sweaty cap. "Thanks. Have a little faith in me. He's nice."

"Why should I have faith in you if you don't?"

His question catches me off guard, but before I can process what he's said, my son's voice rings through the air.

"Mom! Grandpa got me ice cream," Jase yells as he rushes through the dirt and dust toward us with my dad a few paces behind.

"Okay. Stay there," I reply, not wanting him to climb up the bleachers with a cone in one hand. "I'll be right down."

My expression hardens as I turn back to my brother. "What do you mean?"

"If you believed that he was a nice guy...if you had faith, you'd introduce him to Jase."

"I love you, Alec, but shut up. You don't understand."

He lifts his hands in surrender. "Fine. I don't. Just remember, a background check is a call away. Do you want me to give you Steve's number?"

Shaking my head, I work my way down the bleachers as Jase stands at the fence, his little fingers of one hand holding tight to the chain-link fence separating him from home plate while the other hand grasps the dripping cone. His shirt is smeared with melted ice cream and the hand with the cone is quickly disappearing behind a steady drape of white as droplets land on the ground and on his dusty shoes.

"Look at you," I say with a grin. I turn to my dad. "Thanks."

Dad laughs as a half-eaten cone comes to my lips.

"You want some, Mommy?"

I quickly take a small bite, mostly to stop it from hitting my nose. "Yum."

Jase looks out on the field as the teams warm up. "Uncle Alec said he'd take me to the batting cage sometime."

I turn to see Alec who followed me down the stands as he gives me one of his brother-knows-best looks. "You did?" I ask Alec.

"You know, I asked Jase to hang out so that his mommy would have some time for mommy stuff, but apparently, I'm supposed to shut up."

I take a deep breath and let it out. "No background check. Don't push me. I have faith. I just need time." I smile. "And thanks. Jase would love to go to the batting cage."

"It would be a big sacrifice for the women of the world, but maybe after the batting cage..." Alec gets down on one knee and steals a small bite of Jase's ice cream cone. "...we could eat pizza, stay up late at my place, and watch guy movies?" Jase vigorously nods his head as Alec looks up at me with big and pleading eyes, the same color as mine. "On a non-school night of course," he adds.

"Okay," I yield. "You don't suck as a brother."

"Really, we can?" Jase asks.

"The okay was for Uncle Alec," I clarify. "I'm not mad at him anymore. As for spending the night, let's see. And first, your mommy needs a definition of *guy movies* before I even consider it."

"What?" Alec asks dismayed. "Cars and Transformers. Where is your mind, sis?"

Jase bounces to his uncle and gives him a big hug, seeming immune to the stench. I begin to wonder if it's a boy thing. Before I can give it much thought, a giggle rings from my lips as I see the mess Jase has made of Alec's shirt, not that it wasn't bad enough with sweat, but the addition of ice cream makes it worse.

"Did you see me hit it over the fence?" Alec asks Jase.

"I did. Can you teach me to do that?"

"After the way you hit that tomato with the big bat, I'd say it won't be long. Pretty soon I'll be taking lessons from you."

"Really?"

CHAPTER

Sixteen

Malcolm

I grip Mandy's hand tighter as she leads me through the park. As we pass other people, I find myself looking for students from my school or players and parents from the team. The ballfields in the distance are still full of players and spectators, but the open area and playgrounds are beginning to clear out as nighttime settles, the sky steadily growing a richer shade of red as darkness slowly overtakes the blue.

The middle-school soccer team that I'm coaching is actually doing very well. When I'm not preparing for my classroom or talking to—or daydreaming about—Mandy, I've been spending my time learning everything I never knew about soccer. Thankfully, I have great help. Rita Sanchez and her husband are very nice and more than willing to help me learn the finer differences between hockey and soccer. For example, there's no penalty box in soccer, although, sometimes I think it would be a good idea. It also helps that Rita and I share a similar philosophy about the real goal of children's sports. Instead of emphasizing the outcome, we both agree that instilling a love for the game is more important. Even with that philosophy, I'm happy to report that we have a winning record. More important, every student on the team plays. It's about teamwork.

While the athletic director knows my history with the Lightning, to the kids on the team, I'm just the coach. I like that. I like getting to know the players without them giving me a status I no longer deserve. Coaching the team and teaching my class feels a little like my rookie year, needing to prove myself as worthy of my new titles. It's funny how in hockey I was old and now I'm young again.

Holding Mandy's hand is like that...a new start at life...a new life in all aspects, and I'm enthralled.

Still taking in the multitude of faces, I realize that I've never before lived in a town where I might run into people I know. While I like it, I'm not sure I want anyone intruding on the small sliver of time I get to spend with Mandy.

I chuckle to myself, thinking about the last time we were here, parked near the back of the property. Thank God we didn't run into anyone then.

As we move farther and farther from the car, I lean toward Mandy and whisper in her ear, "Are you taking me to the rear parking lot again?" Though I'm partially teasing, I wouldn't complain if her answer is yes. "It might have been better to bring the car, but I do have a blanket in the basket."

"Nope," she says with her magical giggle. "You promised me a picnic. That means the blanket goes on the ground and then there's food in that basket, not a front seat and..."

"Fucking?" I ask, lowering my voice even more. Her cheeks bloom and rise as they fill with pink. Her hair is pulled back in a ponytail, giving me great access to her ear and sensitive skin. I love how casual she looks. It's not like she isn't beautiful all dressed up, but there's something about jeans and a blouse that lets me know she's comfortable with me. Of course, even when she was dressed up, there wasn't much—or anything—I didn't see.

Mandy shakes her head. "Right. None of that."

I swing the picnic basket from my other hand as the breeze rustles the fallen leaves, blowing them into cyclones around our feet. The Midwest is so different from Florida. Down there, it is still essentially summer, despite what the calendar says. Here, everything is changing. It's visible by the way the grass crunches under our shoes and the colorful leaves float through the air. As I take it all in, I'm glad Mandy wanted to do something outside. No loud music or bar scene for her. Instead of a band, the music playing is an orchestra of insects humming as everyday people enjoy life in the distance.

"This is so peaceful," I say.

"It is. I love being outside, especially after being cooped up at work all day."

I lean down and give her a soft kiss on the cheek. "Thanks for coming up with this great idea. Although, for the record, the last time we were here wasn't a bad idea either."

"I'm glad you could come tonight on such short notice," she says, taking us away from the other topic at hand.

Instead of commenting like a teenager on how I want to come, I answer equally as truthfully. "I was thrilled to get your text. I didn't think I'd see you again until later next week."

"My brother surprised me. He planned something special for my son. I couldn't say no."

"So let me get this straight: I get a surprise picnic date, and whatever I come up with for later, you can't say no?" My eyebrows wiggle.

"Whatever could you come up with?" she asks with a sly, knowing grin.

"I'm sure I can come up with something. I could give you the obvious answer, but you just said that the blanket needs to hold the food."

Mandy shakes her head. "For your information, I can say no. And every time I'm not with my son, I feel guilty...but..." Her big light-blue eyes turn my way. "I think in his own way my brother is trying to be sweet. He said this was so I could do mommy stuff. I don't think he meant laundry or grocery shopping."

"Your family sounds very supportive."

"They are." She points up to the trees. With the orange hues of the setting sun, the colors of autumn are more vibrant than only moments earlier. "Aren't the trees beautiful?"

"Is that your way of changing the subject?"

"Yep. Too real. Focus on us."

"Okay," I concede, "but first, I want to say that I'm thankful that your brother is giving us this time."

She squeezes my hand. "Me too."

I stare down at the brunette beauty by my side.

Mandy looks up. "What?"

"I'm just focusing on you."

She shakes her head.

A little later, I lay the blanket over an old wooden table off to the side of the open park. I think it still qualifies as a picnic even if it isn't on the ground and even though I know the rules, the idea of being on the ground with Mandy makes me ready to forget all about food. The trees behind the table give us a little seclusion while open field and lingering sunlight allows us to see. As I place the basket on the table, Mandy rubs her hands together enthusiastically.

"What did you bring?" she asks.

From the basket, I begin to pull out the food I bought at the deli, doing my best Vanna White impression. "For our dining delight...we have chicken, fried and one roasted breast just in case you don't eat fried, coleslaw, pita chips, hummus, and a lovely bottle of sparkling grape juice."

"Grape juice?"

"You said we were coming here. It's not that I'm against breaking a few laws." I raise my brow. "I think we may have the other night. But the city's website said no alcohol in parks. I thought we might be pushing our luck if we tempt fate again so soon. I wanted to be safe. But I do have stronger drinks at home for later."

Mandy continues to pull the paper plates, plastic silverware, and napkins out of the basket. "I love fried chicken, potatoes...just about anything battered and fried," she adds with her cute grin. "And, gosh, Malcolm, this basket is like Mary Poppins's!"

"It does seem to go on forever."

Her blue eyes look my way. "You know Mary Poppins?"

"Of course. Who doesn't? I love Julie Andrews and Dick Van Dyke."

"Don't tell me that you can sing Chim Chim Cher-ee."

"I can, but not well. It would definitely take me drinking something stronger than sparkling grape juice to give it a go."

Mandy's lips surprise mine as she brushes them against my mouth in a soft kiss.

"What was that for?"

"I felt like giving you a kiss. You brought me on a picnic. You made all this food last minute and put it all in these amazing little containers..." She holds up a plastic deli dish. "...and you know Disney."

I reach for her hand and pull her closer. "In the interest of full disclosure, the deli at the superstore made the food, but I did risk life and limb to stand in line to select it and then in another line to purchase it. It took most of my patience to wait behind the reigning state coupon queen."

"I always pick the wrong lane too."

I shake my head. "I had no idea until she pulled out a three-ring binder. At first I was annoyed, but then as the total for her cart full of groceries continued to plummet, I was too impressed. I had to stay to see if the store would pay her to shop."

Mandy laughs. "And...?"

"No, but it was close." I take the container from her hand. "The deli also provided the marvelous containers. But if knowing Disney gets me a kiss, I'll be happy to recite Old Yeller."

"Oh no. You're old school. Besides, everyone knows that movie makes you cry."

"The book too," I say.

Mandy's smile grows. "I love that you read."

"I'm so tempted to ask how many illiterate men you've dated, but I'll stop myself."

"That's good. But the answer is none. It's just that men like... my brother...can read, but they don't read books. It's more like they read sports and car magazines and websites. Ask him anything about the Cubs or Blackhawks and he's all over it."

I stifle the need to wince—another Blackhawks fan.

Instead, without effort the subject moves on.

As we settle at the picnic table and begin eating, we chat about books. I explain how I started reading because I had a job with a lot of travel. I want to tell her about The Lightning Bolts and more, but I keep it generic. I describe how boring it can get on the road. There are always bars. That gets old fast. A lot of other people who I worked with watched movies, but my mom has always been a reader, so I made the mistake of downloading the book app on my phone.

"That doesn't sound like a mistake. I've spent many nights lost in great stories."

"It's one of my favorite ways to go to sleep," I admit.

"How else do you like to fall asleep?" she asks as her eyes open wide.

This time it's Mandy whose smile sends shivers down my spine and straight to my dick.

_I_ stir as Mandy's side of the bed moves.

Before she can get away, I reach for her hand and stop her retreat. "I hate that you sneak out every morning after you stay the night."

"Malcolm?"

"I'm not asking you to choose." I tug her hand so she lands back over me. Her hair falls in waves upon my chest. The dark tresses are no longer secured, but down and messy with the most beautiful case of sex-induced bedhead I've ever seen. I can't stop myself as I reach up and push a piece behind her ear. My touch lingers, allowing my finger to trace the softness of her skin. "I just want you to know that I miss you the moment you leave."

Her head drops to my shoulder. "I-I..."

Reaching for her chin, I bring her lips to mine. Our kiss starts chaste, but within seconds my tongue forgets that she has plans to leave. It probes the seam of her lips for more, and without hesitation she opens and her tongue joins the dance. Her bare tits push toward me as her nipples bead against my exposed chest. It's when the predawn air fills with her moans and whimpers that my morning wood turns to steel.

"A few more minutes?" I ask, peering into her lovely gaze.

Instead of answering, Mandy nods as she lifts herself over me, her petite hands gripping my shoulders as she wiggles her sexy ass above my stomach and allows her luscious tits to swing in front of my face. I can't resist as I lean forward and capture a hard nipple between my lips.

"Oh!"

When my mouth is free, I look up at her and grin. "You asked me yesterday how I like to fall asleep."

"Yeah?"

"I can say without a doubt that this is how I like to wake up."

Mandy giggles, the morning grogginess gone from her tone. "Yes, Malcolm..." She lifts herself over my erection and reaches for my length. Rubbing her hand up and down, she assesses, "...you're definitely up."

My eyes close as she leads me to her entrance and lowers herself, surrounding me, wiggling to bring us closer, stretching her core as her fingernails bite into my shoulders and her back and neck arch. It's once she starts to move that I have to open my eyes to watch her. She's always stunning, but I would say exceptionally so when she falls into the zone: her light-blue eyes staying open wide, staring at me, making me feel as though she wants to be sure I'm still with her as she loses herself to the pleasure.

Once we both find our cliff, we lock hands and jump together without reservation. The free fall goes on and on as I hold her against me.

With her hair in my face and sexy body draped over me, I wrap her tighter in my arms, wanting to say what I've never said before, wanting to tell her how she makes me feel, how I do feel. I want to promise to always be there as she finds that release, how I want to be there for everything, the good and the bad...but I know that isn't what she wants to hear. Not yet. It goes beyond her 'here and now' rules.

I know it does, because I'm most certain that what I'm feeling and the way it's growing stronger by the day is not limited to this moment.

CHAPTER
Seventeen

Amanda

"So?" Sally says, leaning her behind against my desk.

"What?" I ask, my attempt at an innocent stare lost on my closest friend.

"It's been over six weeks. How many times have you seen each other?"

I shrug. "A few."

Sally pushes on my shoulder. "A few. Damn, the nun has left the building."

"I-I." I shift my mouse, bringing my computer screen back to life and deciding if I should answer Cruella or Sally. Looking to my friend, I say, "I think I need to break it off."

"Why?"

"It feels too real."

"What does that even mean?"

"I don't know," I admit, unsure what I want. "It's more than that. It's Jase, too. I feel guilty. He's having some issues with the new school, and I think it's because of me. I've never left him this often before."

"Nonsense," Sally says. "It's not like you leave him alone. When you leave, it's either when Jase is spending the night or after he's gone to bed. He doesn't even know that it's me or your parents with him at night. He's in his bed. You tuck him in and kiss him goodnight. He's never awakened, not once when I've been there. I mean, seriously, that little boy could sleep through an atomic blast."

That makes me giggle. She's right. "I know, but it's not fair to you or Mom and Dad."

"Then invite this mystery man to your place and no babysitters will be necessary."

My lips come together. "No."

Sally lifts her hand in mocked surrender. "Fine. How long do you have to date this guy until we all get to meet him?"

"We're not dating. We're just seeing each other."

"Hmm," she says suspiciously.

"What?"

"I can see how that's so different."

"It is!"

"I get your concern with Jase, but this is me...your best friend. Well," Sally says, "at least you don't have to worry about me hounding you anymore about meeting Pep. According to Brian, he's met someone, someone who..." Her eyebrows wiggle. "...has confirmed that he can get it up."

I scrunch my nose. "That's too much information."

"I don't mean the woman has called Brian and told him that. It's just that Pep is always busy with work or this chick. I'd say you missed out, ex-athlete and all. He didn't get that nickname just because of hockey." She leans back even farther as her hazel stare scans me up and down. "But looking at your satiated smile, I'll bet that you don't care."

"I don't. I'm glad to hear Brian's friend is functional. So is Malcolm."

Sally takes a staggered step away from my desk as her mouth falls open. "What? You've never told me his name before. Are you serious? Is it Malcolm?"

My heart thuds between my spine and ribs, thumping with an unexpected sense of panic. My best friend's complexion has suddenly gone white as a sheet. It's as if she's seen a ghost. "What? Why is that significant?"

"I'm not sure yet. What's his last name?"

"Peppernick. Malcolm Peppernick."

"Fuck!" Sally's hand flies to her lips. "It's you. It's him. You're her! Oh my God, wait until I tell Brian."

"Wait! What? I'm who?"

"Malcolm Peppernick is Pep."

I shake my head, certain she's mistaken. "No. He's not some cocky ex-jock. He's sweet and knows Disney and reads...He can't be..." It's then I realize that Malcolm and I haven't shared our pasts with each other. We've only recently started talking about the present. He knows I work for a financial company. I know he teaches, but I don't even know the grade or subject. I know he agreed to take over as a soccer coach for someone who's ill, but I know that only because he slipped and said something about a game last Saturday. But that's soccer. "I-I...He's never said anything about hockey."

"Amanda!" Cruella de Vil's voice comes from a few cubicles away.

I reach for Sally's hand and speak in a rushed whisper. "Don't tell Brian."

"Why?"

I'm not sure why. I'm just not ready.

"I don't know yet. Just, please." It's the last thing I say before Sally dashes away in hopes of saving Dalmatian puppies or at least in hopes of avoiding the villain in the puppy coat.

---

*M*alcolm reaches for my hand as we enter the restaurant. The dim interior with the background music has become one of my favorite places. There may be another reason I like it. It's where Malcolm and I met.

"What's going on?" he asks.

I take a deep breath and push down my concerns and worries about Jase. He's having more problems with school and his teacher. I've already had one meeting and multiple telephone calls with Mrs. Williams. I wish I could talk to Malcolm about it, but doing that seems like I'm being unfair. I'm not sure to whom —Jase or Jackson or maybe Malcolm. I can't burden him with my problems and still keep him and Jase separated. Instead of talking about that, I concentrate on the surprise Sally and I have planned for Malcolm and Brian. As a rule, I'm not a fan of surprises, but since I'm on the knowing end of this one, I'm excited.

"I told you. We're meeting some friends of mine."

"But you seem...distracted."

As I scan the bar, I look for Brian and Sally. Of course, I don't see them. "Shit. I swear, they're always late."

"I hate that," Malcolm mutters.

My lips tip upward. "Me too."

"Before I went back to college for teaching," Malcolm says, divulging a little bit of his past that he doesn't know I know, "I had a job that required being on time. Arrival times. Scheduled..." He seems to be searching for what is within our rules to say. "...things that needed to be done and places we needed to go. Anyway, you'd be surprised how many supposed adults had trouble with the simple concept of arriving promptly."

"There's a booth," I say, tilting my head toward an open table.

We walk hand in hand. As I ease into the booth, Malcolm follows on the same side. The warmth of his thigh against mine is comforting. I'd say we're sitting close and on the same side because we're meeting Brian and Sally, but we find ourselves this way even when it's only us. It's as if after days apart, the distance across the table isn't simply a few feet, but a chasm neither of us wants to bear.

"I think being late is rude," I say.

Malcolm winks as he reaches again for my hand. "Being on time has been fortuitous in my recent past." He looks around the bar. "At this very establishment, as a matter of fact."

I look down at our entwined fingers and smile. Back up to his eyes, I ask, "Oh, is that so?"

"Yes, you see, I was supposed to meet a *nice* woman, and instead I met—"

"Are you saying I'm not nice?"

"No, beautiful, I'm saying you're the whole fucking package. Now tell me what's bothering you."

How can he, after only a month and half, read me and my feelings so well? "I can't."

"Because whatever it is, it's about your son?"

My chest hurts. I don't want to keep the two most important men in my life separated, but I can't disappoint Jase. I won't introduce him to someone who at any moment could walk away, especially now that he's dealing with new pressures at school. "Yes."

"He's not ill, is he?"

I'm taken aback by the audible concern in Malcolm's tone. "No. It's nothing like that."

"That's good. How old is he?"

"Five," I say with an exaggerated breath.

"Really? What grade is he in? Is he in kindergarten?"

Malcolm's excitement surprises me. "Yes, but it hasn't been an easy transition. I was hoping it would go smoother. I'm afraid I'm the one to blame."

"Why? How are you to blame?"

"My attention has been diverted."

"I wouldn't be so quick to assign responsibility. There are many things that can affect the transition to kindergarten. What's happening, specifically? I know we've agreed not to talk about things too personal such as our jobs, but I work with—"

"No fucking way!" Brian's voice supersedes our conversation.

I break out in laughter as Sally and Brian approach the table, and Malcolm's mouth falls open as he stands up to greet them.

Brian is about Malcolm's age but the exact opposite in appearance. Not as in one is handsome and the other isn't. It's that where Malcolm's hair is dark, Brian's is light, very light, what some would call a towhead. Looking at the two men standing side by side, they're built very similarly: tall, broad shoulders, fit bodies with trim waists and solid chests. It's not hard to believe that they are both former professional athletes.

Sally's smile and her hazel eyes that I adore are shining as brightly as mine. We wink at one another, relishing our success. We'd figured out what neither one of these two men could or did.

"Brian? What the hell are you...?" Malcolm turns toward Sally and extends his hand. "Sally, it's nice to see you again."

"And you too, Pep," my best friend says with a knowing expression.

Malcolm turns toward me. "Pep is an old nickname, short for Peppernick." Malcolm scoots back into the booth next to me as Brian and Sally slide in the other side. Malcolm goes on, "Brian and I played hockey..." His words trail as my smile grows. "You know?" He scans the other faces. Only Brian is as confused as Malcolm appears to be.

"We just figured it out the other day when Amanda finally mentioned your name," Sally explains.

"Wait...these are your friends?" Malcolm asks. "Sally is your friend? You're Sally's friend?"

It's like watching pieces of a puzzle slide together. Like one of those computer games where once the player gets so far and winning is inevitable, the computer does the rest.

Click.

Snap.

Connect.

"Yep," I reply. "We've been friends forever. Actually, she's my best friend."

"Hold up! What does this mean? If you're Sally's friend, then does it mean that I'm..." Malcolm points to himself. "...the poor sap with erection issues?"

We all burst out laughing.

"No, that doesn't seem to be a problem." I whisper my response, hoping that only Malcolm hears, but with the fresh outbreak of laughter and the way my cheeks warm, I'm certain that isn't the case. And then I have the revelation I hadn't thought of before. The other half of the equation hits me. I turn toward Brian. "Hey, that means I'm *nice*, as in uglier than shit?" My eyes open wide and lips purse to the side in a sassy look as I await his response.

"No! I didn't say that," Brian speaks fast. "I said *nice*. I meant nice. Come on, Amanda. You *are* nice."

"Amanda?" Malcolm says. "Of course. I think you may have even said her first name. I didn't fucking put it together."

"What?" Sally asks.

"Mandy is short for Amanda."

Sally's eyes open wide.

I haven't gone by Mandy since Jackson. The only reason I used that name when Malcolm and I first met was because of what my mother had said. Since then, it's stuck.

"Yes, it is," she confirms, eyeing me suspiciously while silently demanding more information.

"Well, fuck," Brian says with a grin. "Let's drink on this new development."

Malcolm nods. "Sure, man, the drinks are on you. You're going to owe me drinks for a long time for telling women I have issues. Hell, I think you'll get the dinner bill too."

Brian shrugs. "I didn't say you had issues. I said I was concerned." He reaches across the table and punches Malcolm's arm. "Friendly concern, that's all." He looks directly at me. "I'm glad to know everything is functional."

My cheeks grow warm again.

"Yep, the nun has left the building," Sally says with a smirk.

The entire table rings with laughter as the waitress arrives to take our order.

CHAPTER
Eighteen

Malcolm

*I*t's been a little over two weeks since Mandy and Sally enlightened Brian and me to the intrigue of Mandy's and my first night. In hindsight, I wonder how we hadn't put it all together. My only excuse is that I was too smitten with Mandy to even consider that she was the *nice* friend of Sally's.

I was wrong when I'd worried that Brian was the same as he was years ago. He's changed too. I'd say we've both grown up. Our time together on the team was as they say 'the time of our life.' While some people find it hard to move on from those kind of glory days, we both seem to have done it. While I went into teaching, Brian went into physical therapy. He still has some more school to finish—right now he's a physical therapy assistant—but he's working as he takes classes to become a physical therapist. Currently, he is working with a center that concentrates primarily on the elderly. He said all those hours spent in ice baths and enduring therapy piqued his interest in the field. He says he owes his ability to walk and rock Sally's world—okay, he hasn't totally changed—to the medical trainers and physical therapists who tended to him and his multiple injuries.

It's a pay-it-forward kind of thing. Now, he wants to do for others what was done for him.

His commitment to his patients is what derailed the blind date. It's why he and Sally never made it to the restaurant. One of the patients whom he sees regularly had an unexpected fall, injuring himself. When Brian got the call, he felt obligated to check on the elderly man.

Who would have suspected under our slick playboy exteriors there were grown men who could handle real responsibilities?

Now that we've all reconnected, Brian and mostly Sally, helped me to nearly accomplish a miracle. Okay, maybe it's not a miracle. Those are miraculous feats like virgin births and turning water into wine. However, if you ask me, this is close.

I'm very close to accomplishing a never previously attempted feat of gigantic proportions. I'm taking Mandy with me for a weekend out of town. I understand her commitment to her son, but I think she deserves a weekend away, full of fun and pampering. Thankfully, I'm not the only one who feels that way.

The way I see it, Mandy shouldn't always be the one who takes care of other people. There's no way I could have made it work without Sally's help. It's rather hilarious how Sally ganged up with Mandy's mother to help me pull this off.

The still yet to be seen part is Mandy's reaction to it all: she doesn't know what's happening yet. She thinks we're meeting Sally and Brian again for dinner. She's right, but what she doesn't know is that the dinner is in Tampa, as in Florida.

The Lightning Bolts are having a special pregame ceremony on Saturday night. It's the anniversary of the season when we won the Stanley Cup. This ceremony, bringing back members of the championship team, is supposed to be good luck for the season ahead. It doesn't hurt for PR purposes either. It isn't my thing, but it gave me a reason to whisk her away.

I glance over to see Mandy looking around as we pull onto the street that leads to the airport. There really isn't much else in this vicinity. She has to suspect something.

"Malcolm, where are we? I thought we were meeting Sally and Brian."

"We are."

I slow as we approach the short-term parking garage.

"At the airport? Why would we have dinner here?"

The gray skies overhead are the reason for her coat and gloves, but where we're going, she'll be able to show off her sexy body in sundresses and bathing suits.

"Well, you see, dinner isn't for another few hours."

"What?"

"But if you're hungry, I think we have time to grab an appetizer and drink before we leave."

Mandy is sitting straighter. Her neck is flexing in that way I've learned it does when she's suddenly nervous or worried. I reach out and touch her thigh. "Don't worry. It's a surprise."

Her lips purse as her head slowly shakes. "No. I don't like surprises."

"You'll like this one...I hope."

After the gate lifts to the parking garage and I take the little ticket, I continue driving around the circular lot, getting higher and higher until I find a parking space. The entire time I feel her stare on me. "Green three," I say aloud.

Her head is now shaking vigorously back and forth. "No. I need to be home in the morning. My mom—"

I seize her petite hand, stilling her words. "Your mom knows. Sally helped. Your mom isn't expecting you until Sunday evening. Sally packed your suitcase."

"What? No." Her voice grows louder. "This is ludicrous. You can't kidnap me. I need to be home for Ja—my son."

"And you will be, on Sunday before he goes to bed. I'm not kidnapping you. There's no ransom note. And you can't be kidnapped if I plan to return you on Sunday. I'm simply borrowing you."

Mandy takes a deep breath with her eyes still too wide. "You could have asked."

"I could have, but I think you would have told me no."

"I would have. I've never, *never* in his whole life left my son for two days."

"Then it's time."

"No! You don't understand..."

I lean forward and stop her protest with a gentle touch of my palm to her cheek, pulling her moving lips my direction and swallowing her words with a kiss. When she finally seems to relax—if only a smidgen—her body melting my way, I speak, "I don't. I don't understand. Not because I don't want to understand, but because you haven't shared. Let me tell you what I do understand?"

"Malcolm."

I touch a finger to her perfectly kissable lips. "Shh, please?"

She nods against my finger.

"Brian and I are part of a pregame ceremony tomorrow night in Tampa—"

"Tampa! No!" She gets the words out before I can touch her lips again with the tip of my finger.

"...in Tampa," I go on. "Sally is coming with Brian. I wish I could say it was my idea to bring you, but it was her idea that we all go." I continue talking before Mandy can protest more. "Sally made the arrangements with your parents. I know you haven't introduced me to them, and I get it. I thought it would be a bit presumptuous of me to show up at their house, introduce myself, and explain that I wanted to borrow you for the weekend."

A smile threatens Mandy's scowl as the tips of her lips fight the urge to smile. "My dad might have hurt you."

That makes me smile. "If I were your father, I'd probably do the same. So you see why it worked better this way. You're here and I'm unharmed by a crazed, overprotective father."

"I think my brother might be more of a threat."

"I'll keep that in mind."

She shakes her head. "So my mom knew about this?"

"Yes, she helped Sally with your packing and agreed to keep your son."

Mandy reaches for her phone. Before she dials, I put my hand over hers and say, "You're only allowed one call."

"What? Am I under arrest?"

"One call, Ms. Wells. Okay, one call per day. Who will it be?"

"Will I see Sally?"

"Yes, they're supposed to be here already."

She laughs. "Which means they're not."

I nod my agreement.

"My mom."

I release her hand with her phone.

I haven't met her mom, but as the phone call ensues, I decide that I like her. Not only did she help with getting Mandy away for this weekend, but as soon as the call connects, her mother's laughter rings out from the phone, filling the interior of my car. It's nice to know that Mandy has so much support.

After the initial laughing, I can only hear Mandy's side of the conversation. "...knew? Why didn't you say anything? ...Yes, I know that's how surprises work. You know I hate surprises... What about...?" Her eyes dart to me.

It admittedly hurts more and more that she won't even say her son's name in front of me, but I can't change that. What I can do is hope that one day she'll trust me more, and in the meantime, I can give her an unforgettable weekend.

Mandy's still speaking. "I didn't tell him goodbye. ...Okay. Tell him I love him. Tell him I'll call tomorrow." Her gaze darts back to me. No doubt she's thinking about her one call restriction. "And it may be on Sally's phone, so be sure to answer."

I just shake my head. Damn, she's a handful and I love it.

"Because...I'm not sure if you packed my charger. Oh, you did... You don't know," she says, "I mean, Malcolm could be a serial killer, and you packed my bag!"

Her tone is lighter than it's been and it makes me smile.

"And you trust Sally? ...I hope I see you again on Sunday.... I love you too, Mom. Bye."

After she disconnects, she stares down at her phone for a minute and then back to me. "I don't know how you did it."

"With help." I reach for her hand. "You didn't let me finish about what I understand."

"Fine. What do you understand?"

"That you've rocked my world. I understand that you have a son and responsibilities." I nod toward her phone. "And that you have a super support system. I don't fully understand why I can't know them. I mean, I do get it...but as I've said, I'll take what I can get, what you're willing to give. Right now, I'm getting your undivided attention for an entire weekend."

"Minus phone calls," she interjects.

"Minus one call per day. Today's is done. Don't make me take your phone away."

Her pretty eyes narrow. "You wouldn't dare."

I lift my brows. "Something that you might want to understand about me: I love a challenge. And what you just said feels like a gauntlet being thrown down, a proverbial line in the sand— Florida sand in this case."

"Fine." Mandy takes a deep breath. "I won't call, but I have to have my phone in case my mom or dad needs to call me."

"Deal," I say, extending my hand. After we shake, I watch as the front of her jacket rises and falls and imagine only a light top, sundress, or bathing suit. Hell, maybe warmer climates are better. "Now that we're on the same page, are you ready for an adventure?"

Mandy leans forward and places her palm on my cheek. "Malcolm Peppernick, I want to be mad at you, but how can I be mad when you went to all this trouble to steal me away?"

"You can't," I agree.

"I've never been kidnapped before. Oh," she says, her tone feigning duress. "Whatever is going to happen to me?"

I reach for her hand and kiss the soft skin of her palm. "I plan to return you Sunday night, perhaps a little sore and worn out, but only because all your wildest fantasies have been fulfilled."

"It's been a long time since I've entertained fantasies."

"Then it's past time to start. Let's get out of this car, go through security, and get something to eat. I doubt your fantasies include starvation."

Her eyes widen. "It depends on the cause. A plane crash on a desert island—no. But...that first night when we almost forgot to eat our pizza—that was an acceptable reason for starvation."

"Oh, but, beautiful, I didn't forget to eat."

Mandy shakes her head as pink fills her cheeks in an endearing way. As we get out of my car and I open the trunk, she says, "Hey, that's my suitcase."

"Because you're going on a weekend getaway."

"Oh, yeah."

"And we're not flying over any deserted islands, so no worries."

"Good to know."

CHAPTER
Nineteen

Mandy

$\mathcal{T}$he roar of the engines has muted to a constant drone as I look around the airplane's cabin. Sally is looking at me with a big shit-eating grin on her face as she leans forward from the other side of the aisle and lifts her glass of wine my direction. I've already told her that I hate her and I'm never speaking to her again, but it doesn't stop me from lifting my glass to her in an air toast.

Malcolm squeezes my hand. "Are you all right? I had no idea you've never flown before."

My shoulders move up and down. "Again, you could have asked."

He bends down and plants a kiss on my cheek. "I just did. Are you all right?"

"Well, other than never speaking to my best friend or mother again, I think I'm all right." I turn and look out the small window. Above the clouds the sun is still shining. As the plane heads south, the sun is moving lower toward the western horizon, casting an amazing array of red, orange, and pink hues through the sky, their shimmers reflecting off the tops of the clouds.

I never really thought about the other side of clouds—the top side. Unlike their underside, which is often gray, the tops are a marvelous mountain range composed of magnitudes of different depths, some as tall as Denali while others appear as cavernous as the Grand Canyon. As we move over them I conjure stories I can tell Jase about mountains of marshmallow fluff. That's exactly what it looks like—fluff. "It's like," I say, "like nothing I ever imagined."

The four of us are in first class, filling both sides of the aisle. And I can't stop my glee as I settle against the soft leather seat. When Malcolm first told me what was happening, I was mad. I was upset, but once I gave in to the reality of my 'kidnapping'— quotes are purposeful—it made everything more exciting.

When we arrived at the airport, my ticket was already on Malcolm's phone. All it took was showing my ID, checking our bags, and walking through security. Then the next thing I knew, we were sitting at a small airport bar waiting for Sally and Brian as we sipped white wine and ate fried pickles.

You would think being married to a man in the military I would have flown, but I never did. Jackson left for basic training before we were married. Our wedding ceremony was between his training and deployment. If he'd been deployed stateside, I would have gone. That probably would have meant driving, but I would have gone. As it was, moving to my own place was the only independence I experienced. It wasn't my own place, but ours. A small apartment, even smaller than the one I now share with Jase. Though it belonged to both of us, I was there alone while he was overseas.

At the time, I thought I was grown up with my own space. Truthfully, I had yet to be inducted into adult responsibilities.

While Jackson was protecting our country, I was working and taking classes. I missed out on the support of other army wives by not living near a base, but I didn't want to leave my parents or his parents to live near strangers, even if they would have a better understanding of what I was going through. In hindsight, I think that was the right decision.

Jackson was home for three months between deployments. That was our most normal feel at married life. During that time, he worked for a recruiting center while awaiting his next assignment. We had hopes for stateside orders and dreams of playing house. That's why we agreed to start a family.

And then things happened overseas. I follow the news, but I still don't think the public is given all the information. The army asked for volunteers to go back to the zones, soldiers who knew the terrain. If they didn't get the number of soldiers they needed via volunteers, they would have chosen them anyway. I think it was one of those requests that you really can't refuse.

I'm not insinuating that the military is like the mafia, but...

We didn't find out that I was pregnant until after the paperwork was signed. By then it was too late. The army didn't assign Jackson a wife. He'd taken one on his own. We'd heard that before. His assignment was only supposed to be for twelve months. The pay was higher than he'd made before due to the increased risk. He'd been there before and had returned. We both thought it would be worth it. Once his second deployment was over, we had visions of a nest egg to live on while we both were able to work on our education. With both sets of parents close by, we knew we'd have help with our growing family.

Jackson flew home the week before my due date. According to Alec, who was also in the same unit in Iraq, Jackson did everything he could do to get home. He took every duty, begged every favor, and pulled every possible string. All I know was that he was with me when we welcomed Jason Mathew Harrison into the world. I watched the wonder in my husband's eyes as he held his son for the very first time.

Jackson only had three months left in Iraq, and then our future would begin.

If he chose to keep going with the enlistment after he returned, we were guaranteed stateside. I had dreams of living in a warm state, playing house with my husband and son, and even flying home to our parents for the holidays.

That never happened.

"You're far away again," Malcolm says as he caresses my thigh.

"I was just thinking about flying. I always wanted to."

"Good. I hope we can come up with a few other things you always wanted to do this weekend."

I take a deep breath and concentrate on the handsome man beside me. "Tell me about Saturday night. Are you and Brian like superstars or heroes?"

"No. My dad served in the military..." Malcolm's words sting my heart, yet there's no way for him to know what I'm thinking. "...those men and women are heroes. Brian and I were overpaid kids who enjoyed getting knocked around and knocking others around on the ice."

There's something in his self-deprecating statement that makes Malcolm even more special than he's ever been. I recall how the boy in Jase's preschool was negative toward soldiers. Malcolm and I have never discussed our military, but if his opinions were different, I know it would have an influence on mine. I don't expect us to agree on everything, but in my opinion the military isn't political: it's simply people working hard and risking their lives. And those people deserve our respect.

"Overpaid kids," I finally say. "I'm surprised more people don't sign up for that kind of gig."

"Oh, it sounds appealing, especially to a testosterone-filled young man. But the truth is that that job can only be maintained for so long and then the body gives out."

That makes me smile. I tilt my head to the side and give Malcolm an up-and-down scan and finally a wink. "I'm pretty sure from what I've seen that your body is still doing okay."

"Okay? Gee, thanks for the compliment. It's a real boost for my morale."

"Better than okay," I say, motioning toward Brian and Sally who are laughing and making out like the hormonal teenagers Malcolm was describing. "Tell me we're not sharing a room with those two."

"Oh no, beautiful Mandy, I plan to have you all to myself."

He looks toward the window. "I wish we were arriving before dark. The sunsets off the Gulf Coast of Florida are some of the best in the world. I haven't traveled far and wide, but I can personally boast that they can be spectacular. It's as if you see the big red ball of fire hit the water. My mom used to say it sizzles. As the sky and clouds filled with reds and pinks, she'd tell us to be quiet and listen to the sizzle."

"Us?" I ask, knowing I'm breaking my own rule.

"I have a sister and brother." Malcolm leans closer. "Can I tell you more?"

"Are the three of you close?"

"They live in different states, but we all get together with our parents for holidays and special occasions. We talk on the phone."

"Do they know about me?"

"Yes."

I nod, wanting to ask more, wondering what he's said, but at the same time, I'm afraid that if I do, it will make whatever this is too real. Instead, I change the subject. "What about tomorrow?"

"Tomorrow?"

"I mean the sunset. We could watch it tomorrow..." And then I remember. "Oh, we'll be at the hockey game?"

He nods. "I guess that means only one thing."

"And what would that be?"

"This will have to be our first trip to Florida. I need to bring you back so you can see a sunset."

I don't argue. I'm already so far beyond my plans for one night. I don't know what to think as I settle back against the seat and enjoy the warmth of Malcolm's hand on my thigh. As I do, I realize that part of me wants to believe there could be another time and another trip. For only a moment, I allow myself the small fantasy of expectancy.

Malcolm had said this weekend was to explore my fantasies.

You would think that my fantasies would include crazy sex or money to burn, but they don't. To me a fantasy is a reprieve from the weight of the world and the luxury of allowing myself to want something in the future, to even go as far as to expect it. That's something I rarely do—expect anything...or hope for more—but since this one weekend is supposed to be about my fantasies, I let myself go.

I just need to remind myself what it is.

A fantasy. Not reality.

"It's absolutely stunning," I say as I stand on the balcony of our room overlooking the water. Though the sun has set, the moon's rays create a silver cast over the waves. The silver-coated darkness goes on forever, with only the lights of a few ships in the distance. "I've never seen the ocean before either."

Malcolm shakes his head. "I wish I could tell you that this is it."

I look out over the darkness and take it all in: the swoosh of gentle waves, a warm breeze, and the scent of salt filling my senses. "What do you mean?"

"This is a bay, Tampa Bay, off the Gulf of Mexico. We would need to travel to the other side of the state for an ocean."

I reach for his hand. "No more traveling. I want to stay here. Whatever that is, it's big and it's saltwater. I can pretend."

"You're absolutely stunning." He tucks a rogue strand of my hair behind my ear. "I hope you know that."

I look down. The dress I'm wearing is the blue sundress from our first date, the beginning of my one night. I was so glad to see it packed with my other things that I almost cried. I can hardly believe that it's mid-October and I'm standing outside in a sundress in warm air. "I-I don't..."

Malcolm wraps his arms around my waist and pulls me close. Our hips unite as my breasts smash against his chest. I have to crane my neck upward to see him—not that I can truly see him in the darkness, but I see his features: his brow, his cheeks, his nose, and his lips...

"Thank you, Mandy, for allowing me to kidnap you. I know we aren't talking about too much personal information, but you now know about my history with the Lightning Bolts. I've avoided these kinds of things—these ceremonies and accolades—since I retired. I probably would have avoided this one also if it weren't for Sally suggesting you come along too.

"I gave it some thought and hoped that if I took you away— brought you here—you'd let me do what you won't allow me to do at home."

I lean back to see his eyes. "And what exactly do you mean?"

Malcolm's chuckle eases my wayward thoughts. "Spoil you. That's what I mean."

"You do. You have. You don't need to. This is all so new."

His chin settles over the top of my head, tucking me against his broad chest. I nestle my cheek against his shirt and wrap my arms around his waist. The swish of the waves in the distance, the steady beat of his heart, and the scent of his cologne dominate my senses.

"You're such a mystery." His words rumble through me. "You're the strongest, most determined woman I've ever met, and at the same time, I'm awestruck by your innocence."

"Hey..."

"No, beautiful, that's not a bad thing. I meant it as a compliment." He turns to the sound of the surf from the bay. "I wanted to take you away this weekend to spoil you with a fancy hotel, expensive dining, massages, a limo ride to the game, the exclusive Lightning executive suite... I wanted to show you how special you are to me, and yet, an airplane ride and a beach, and you're happy."

"I am," I say. "I don't need all that other stuff."

"God, you're so much more than I ever knew I wanted."

My heart tugs. I can't make Malcolm promises because I am more. I'm not a single woman who can be whisked away. I'm more than me. I'm Jase too. "Malcolm, can we live in the moment?"

He reaches for my hand and leads me back into the hotel room. "Yes...in case you didn't notice, we have our very own Jacuzzi spa in the bathroom. I say we start living there, and then the moment can come out here to the king-sized bed...the one where you won't get up and leave me at daybreak. And if you want, we can take the moment to the balcony or the beach..."

I giggle. "Let's keep those moments in here for now. And no, I won't be leaving at daybreak. If I recall, I'm being held captive until Sunday night."

"That's right. The entire weekend where you're all mine."

"With a limited phone plan."

Malcolm's smile is inviting as he tugs my hand. "Come this way...we have moments to live."

My breasts vibrate with laughter as he pulls me through the bathroom door, my bare feet sliding on the shiny tile. The tub is huge. "I'd say I've never been in a tub that big before, but you're getting a big head with all these firsts."

Malcolm's eyes widen. "It's not my head that's growing at this moment. Well..." His laugh resonates through the bathroom as he adjusts the water in the spa to warm. When he turns back to me, his blue eyes are darkened with desire. Reaching for the straps of my dress, his finger teases my skin. "Maybe this time we can save the dress?"

"What about my panties?"

"No, beautiful. They're goners."

CHAPTER
Twenty

Mandy

I feel like the words are redundant at this point when I say *I've never done this before*, but as I hold tightly to Malcolm's arm and he walks me into the Lightning Bolt's executive suite high above the ice at Amalie Arena, I'm having a hard time coming up with anything else to say. All of the attention his mere presence garners leaves me a bit speechless.

The actual arena is gigantic, like a football stadium. Malcolm would say football stadiums are like hockey stadiums, but again, this is new to me. The executive suite reminds me of a man cave on steroids. Couches and chairs in clusters, a large kitchen area with an island full of food, and a bar with two bartenders ready for anything. There are some regular tables and other tall ones for standing. Beyond the perimeter is a balcony with more seats and ledges that overlook the rink. If perhaps we decided we didn't want to watch the game live, it appears it will be playing on one of the many giant screens throughout the suite.

Sally reaches over and pinches my elbow. "Isn't this cool?" Her excitement mirrors my own.

I nod my agreement as Malcolm stops to talk to some other men in suits. They all look very handsome, tall, and fit, but as I eye his ex-teammates, I find myself more enthralled with the one whose arm I'm holding.

"...introduce you to my girlfriend, Mandy Wells."

Pink fills my cheeks as I reach out and shake each person's hand. At first I have to fight the urge to redefine myself. I've never thought of myself as Malcolm's girlfriend. Does that make him my boyfriend? Do I have a boyfriend? When does one become too old to have boyfriends and girlfriends?

As all those questions run through my head, I'm trying to keep track of names. The most consistent comment from his ex-teammates is astonishment that Pep has one girlfriend.

"Nice to meet you, Mandy. I never thought I'd see the day when Pep settled down. You must be quite the woman."

I simply smile and nod, not knowing exactly how to respond. Thankfully, Malcolm saves me from most, answering for me. "She is...I couldn't be happier." With each response, my contentment grows.

About a half hour before the game, things change. Malcolm gives me a kiss on the cheek, and I know he's about to leave for his ceremony.

"Beautiful, don't you dare go home with anyone else while I'm gone," he whispers. "I see them looking at how gorgeous you are."

"I didn't know that was an option. I've never been kidnapped by someone famous before."

"It's not."

"Then I'll be right here."

That earns me a quick squeeze of my hand and a wink.

Within minutes the suite is much less crowded with the noticeable absence of over a half-dozen tall, wide, and handsome men. That leaves us with a few couples and many women, some of whom look much more comfortable in an executive suite than I feel.

"I'm so glad you're here," Sally says as we make our way toward the food bar.

"I don't think I had a choice."

"But now that you're here..."

"It's fun," I confess.

She gives me a wink. "See, I knew you could do it."

"What, come to a hockey game?"

"No, have fun and live a little."

I shrug. "I feel guilty about this entire weekend. I'm sure Jase is fine, but I've never left him."

"And when you're doing that living thing..."

"I admit this is really neat."

We take our plates and drinks and move out onto a balcony that overlooks the rink. My skin pebbles with goose bumps. Even with the air conditioning in the suite, it's cooler over the ice. "I know I keep saying firsts, but this is my first hockey game," I say casually as we watch our men from high above. They're near the side of the ice by what appears to be an announcer's table.

"Hmm. Pathetic."

Sally and I both turn to the tall blonde woman beside us.

"Excuse me?" Sally asks. "Did you say something?"

"I said pathetic. Pep finally decides to settle down and you've never seen him play? You probably don't know his stats or his number. You've probably never slept in his jersey or stood in line for an autographed picture."

"Umm." I'm admittedly a little taken aback.

"No, she doesn't need to do any of those things—not with him on her arm," Sally replies, her big-sister act in full gear. "And why should she sleep in his jersey when she has *him* in her bed?"

"Well, don't think it will last. There's not one of us in here who hasn't been in his bed. He doesn't stick around long, so enjoy it while you can. Tomorrow you'll be yesterday's news."

Sally takes a step closer to the woman. "Just because you're discarded trash stinking up the sidewalk doesn't mean everyone is."

"Well!" the tall blonde says with a huff as she walks back to a group of women.

"Don't listen to her," Sally whispers.

I put my plate down on the small ledge, my appetite waning. "This—this is why—"

"No, stop that right now. Do you think Pep is interested in a woman like that?"

"It sounds as though he was."

Sally shakes her head and then diverts my attention to the ice. "Look!"

The giant arena has gone dark, except for multiple circles of light flashing from side to side. There is music blaring as an announcer begins to speak in a deep, booming voice.

"It's our pleasure..." the PA system shouts. "...to reintroduce from the two thousand and..." The crowd cheers so loudly that I make a mental note to ask Malcolm what year they're celebrating. "...Stanley Cup champions!" More cheering, and then the lights all come together in a giant circle in the middle of the rink, highlighting a blue bolt of lightning. And then, one by one the teammates come forward as they announce their names. To my surprise they don't announce Malcolm as Malcolm Peppernick, but as Pep Peppernick.

"I guess he really did go by that name?" I whisper rather loudly to be heard in Sally's ear.

She nods. "He did. Haven't you Googled him or anything?"

"No." My answer makes me feel guilty. I don't know who he is. Or maybe I do...I know the real man—who he is now. Not the man he was. I know that he's Malcolm Peppernick, the handsome gentleman who whisked me off my feet, pursued me, and has given me all the space and time that I've asked for—except for this weekend of kidnapping.

Sally and I cheer as Malcolm and Brian are announced. For a second it reminds me a little of high school when Jackson and Alec's names were announced over the loudspeaker. And then, I take in the size of Amalie Arena and concede that this is a much bigger scale. I also imagine that if Alec were here, he might think that Malcolm is an all-right guy.

Ignoring the other women, Sally and I sit as the game begins. I should know something about hockey, but except that the goal is to get the puck in the net—aptly called the goal—I'm lost. I know baseball, football, and basketball. Using context clues, I try to follow the game. Maybe it's the blonde's comment that may have bothered me. I should know more about the game.

It doesn't take long to realize the Bolts are the ones in blue, which is the exact opposite of football where the home team always wears white. I'm mesmerized by the intensity as they play. The players are giving it one hundred and ten percent as their skates sail and ice chips fly. In football, there's a pause after each play. This game just seems to continue at full speed. It isn't until a large hand covers my shoulder and a deep voice whispers in my ear that I totally forget about the blonde's comment. Maybe it isn't gone, but with Malcolm beside me, I no longer care.

"Hi, beautiful. Did you miss me?"

"Yes," I reply with a kiss.

Before the game is over, Malcolm offers to take me on a walk around the arena. It seemed big from the outside, but from within, it's mammoth. Everywhere we go, people stare. One little boy even stops us and asks Malcolm for his autograph.

"Do they still make your jersey?" I ask once we have a moment alone.

The endearing pink that I saw the first night at the bar comes back to his cheeks as he shakes his head. "Mandy, no. That isn't why I brought you here. I hoped you'd have fun, but honestly, this isn't my idea of fun any longer."

"According to some tall, buxom blonde, you have quite the reputation."

"I don't give a shit about any tall blonde. Do you know whose opinion I care about?"

"The little boy who just wanted your autograph?"

"Well, I wouldn't want to disappoint that kid, but no. I only care about yours, a petite, ravishing brunette. If this place makes you uncomfortable—because it no longer feels like home to me—then we can leave."

"We can stay. I like learning about you."

"I thought we weren't supposed to get too real."

I shrug. "Who I'm learning about isn't really you. That's what I realized after that woman spoke. The Pep who she talked about isn't you. It's who you used to be. It's like a history lesson."

"When do I get to learn your history?"

My expression falls before I can pretend it doesn't.

Malcolm leans close and kisses my nose. "I'm not asking. You didn't ask either. I brought you here. When you're ready to share, I'm here."

I nod as I take a deep breath. My fingers splay over the buttons of his shirt. "This is you." I press my hand against his chest. "This is the Malcolm I know. As long as he's with me, I'm happy to stay." Out of the corner of my eye I see a group of boys who look only slightly older than Jase staring our direction. "I think you have a fan club over there."

"How about when this is over, I take the person whose fan club I'm the head of back to the hotel and we take a moonlit walk on the beach?"

"I thought we had some big dinner..."

"Beautiful, I have to give you back tomorrow night. I don't want to share you with a room full of people, especially ego-inflated jocks and ex-jocks. Honestly, I've had enough of this reunion."

I nod. "Okay. I need to let Sally know."

Malcolm turns and smiles at the growing group of boys. I stand back and watch as he kneels down on one knee and talks and teases.

"Are you really Pep?" one asks nervously.

"I am..."

"Did you really...?"

I can't help but compare the boys to Jase. If Malcolm is this attentive with little boys he doesn't know, how would he be...?

No. I remind myself that what I'm imagining can't happen. It's just that this weekend of fantasies is going to my head.

*H*olding the straps of my sandals, I walk barefoot through the soft sand with Malcolm. Along the shore and going on forever are lights from all the hotels and restaurants. In the breeze is the distant din of people partying and enjoying the beautiful atmosphere. My hair and dress fly backward from the breeze and I need to lift my chin to keep my hair out of my eyes.

Malcolm takes ahold of my other hand as we walk together, enjoying the silence as much as our conversations. The damp sand squeezes between my toes as the warm water laps over my feet.

"Thank you," I finally say.

"For what? I feel like maybe tonight was a bust. I'm sorry about—"

I lift myself up on my toes and stop his apology with a kiss. I meant it to be quick, but with the way his large hand grabs hold of my waist and pulls me against him, I don't want to back away. Instead, I melt against him, hoping my body can tell him what my mind won't allow my words to say.

"Mandy, you're so much more than those women. I hope you can see that."

"I really can't. But I can see that you think so, and that's enough for me...for right now." I add the end to remind myself that this is a weekend escape, not real life. "The thank-you I gave you is for kidnapping me. It's my first kidnapping, and I think I like it."

"So many firsts," he says with a grin. "I'm glad you like it." His eyes shimmer with reflections of the distant lights. He pulls me closer, our hips uniting, wordlessly letting me know that if I'm game, we could go back to the room and live a few more moments.

"I do," I answer with an equally big smile. "I do like it, as long as you don't mind that I still call you Malcolm." I scrunch my nose. "Pep is cute, but I prefer Malcolm."

"I especially like to hear my name when you scream it...you know, with sailor talk before and after."

I shake my head as he reaches for my hand, and we head back to the hotel.

CHAPTER
Twenty One

Malcolm

Streaks of color crack open the gray night skies in a kaleidoscope of hues as the early rays of dawn's lights prepare for another day. Quietly sliding open the door, I sneak out onto the balcony and into the gentle, early breeze as I leave Mandy sleeping soundly in the king-sized bed. Before I left the room, I couldn't stop myself from watching her sleep, so serene and carefree in her dreams. I've seen her fall asleep before. I've heard her cute short breaths and seen her lovely lips opened slightly as her hair lies sexily mussed over her pillow. However, usually that's at night, not as the sun is rising.

I wanted to rouse her, pull her toward me, and begin our day in my new favorite way to wake, but lingering thoughts over last night combined with her obvious state of slumber-induced contentment wouldn't allow me to disturb her.

It isn't often, or ever, that Mandy stays at my apartment beyond sunrise. Having her with me for an entire weekend has been everything I'd hoped it would be. And yet, as I stand outside on the concrete balcony, instead of allowing myself to revel in the positive, I can't help but think about the incident with the blonde bimbo at the arena and worry that with a few words, that woman nearly ruined everything.

Mandy barely mentioned the woman and what she said—only something about my having a reputation. It was Sally who filled me in on the extent of the woman's remarks before Mandy and I went on our walk around Amalie. Once we were alone, I apologized to Mandy and offered to take her back to our room. Though she didn't seem upset, I definitely am.

When I told Mandy that she's so much more than that woman or others like her, I meant it with my whole heart. I know from experience that if someone would have approached one of those women like that one did Mandy, a catfight would have ensued. I wouldn't be surprised if that was what the blonde was after.

Mandy is so much more...so above that kind of behavior.

It's refreshing and endearing and part of the reason that as rays of sunlight begin to fill the sky, I'm outside instead of in the bed beside her. Mandy's reaction may be refreshing, but it's also foreign and completely contradictory to the behavior of the women I used to see.

Part of me is concerned that she's more upset than she let on. That her mild response is simply a cover and when we return home, Mandy will tell me to go back to the women of hockey.

That isn't even an option.

I couldn't. I won't.

I'm out of my element. As a man who had his way with any woman he never wanted...I'm at a loss as to what to do with the one I want more than anything in the world.

Leaning my elbows on the rail of our private balcony, I watch the sky as the sun rises behind me, casting a shadow of the hotel upon the sand, its definition becoming clearer with each minute of light. Above the shallow waters flocks of seagulls fly, scanning the blue surface until one or more plunges deep into the sea in search of its breakfast. At the same time, hordes of sandpipers peck the beach in search of their morning meals.

"What are you doing?"

I didn't hear Mandy approach until her question comes to me and warm, soft arms surround my waist from behind. Within seconds, Mandy's cheek settles against the cotton of my T-shirt stretched across my back, pressing the front of her body against me—together yet still too far apart.

Slowly, I stand straighter and turn, not wanting to break our connection while allowing her arms to stay around me. Once we're facing each other, I take her in. Though I'd thrown on a T-shirt and pair of basketball shorts before leaving the room, to my delight Mandy is wearing only the soft white robe with the hotel's emblem on the lapel. While grasping her arms, I hold her out to arm's length and take her in, conspicuously scanning her scrumptious body. My gaze moves from her bare toes—wiggling upon the concrete floor—up her shapely legs—the ones I love having wrapped around me—to the place I love to be buried—that's unfortunately covered with terrycloth, an evil sash around her waist keeping the robe in place—to the swell of her barely visible breasts, and higher still to her defined collarbone and long slender neck. By the time my eyes reach her gorgeous face, her cheeks hold the endearing pink I adore, and her lips are curved into a bashful grin. It's as our eyes meet and her light-blue ones sparkle with the day's early light that my knees grow weak.

"I'm..." I'm not sure what to say about last night, about today...what to profess that won't scare her away from me forever.

"You're...?" she asks.

"I didn't want to wake you."

She lessens the distance as she pulls herself closer, her cheek tucked against my chest as my chin fits on top of her head. "I like when you wake me."

"I'm sorry." It seems insufficient. For a teacher—a man who has studied language—I'm at a loss for words.

Mandy looks up until our gazes meet. "Why?"

My Adam's apple bobs as I try to come up with an explanation.

She leans back even farther, her expression of contentment fading as her brow furrows. "Malcolm, please talk to me."

"I'd rather pick you up and throw you on the bed...wake you the way we both enjoy."

She shakes her head. "We're already out here and awake. Why

are you sorry? Do you wish you wouldn't have brought me? Kidnapped me?"

"No." I pull her hips closer to mine. "I wish I could kidnap you forever." Before her eyes fill with that battle between me and her responsibilities, I add, "I'd be happy to kidnap all of you."

"I think you did."

"No, Mandy, *all* of you...means more than you. But," I say quickly, "I know you're not ready for that, and I won't push. I refuse to lose you because you feel pressured or because of something some bimbo says—"

Her eyes open wide. In the new day's light, they match the soft hue of the sky over the bay.

"Is that why you're out here? Is that why you're apologizing?" Each one of her questions grows in volume. "Because of *that* woman?"

I simply nod.

"Malcolm, don't give her that much credit. I'm not. I gave up childish behavior when I had a child. I said that I was okay. That woman is petty and jealous and..." She leans back and gives me the same scan I gave her earlier. Once she reaches my eyes, her smile grows. "...besides, I'm with you. We've been together for longer than one night, and I don't feel like you want to discard me, like she said—"

"I don't."

She shakes her head again. "I don't have time in my life for petty. I don't have time in my life for kidnapping either..." She lifts herself up on her toes and kisses my cheek. "...but I made an exception. So please don't worry that I'll be jealous of your past." For a split second, a shadow passes behind her beautiful stare. And then it's gone, and she continues, "I'm impressed with all you've shown me and proud to be with you. I...want to give you more...I do. But it takes me time. I guess if I can ask anything, it's that you be patient. You have been, but don't stop."

I lean down and kiss her forehead. "I won't stop if you won't stop. I have plenty of time."

"Then in the meantime, let's not spend that time apologizing for someone else. Besides, Sally shot her down."

"Yeah," I say with a grin. "Sally's the one who told me all that was said."

"Then did Sally tell you how upset I was and how I threatened to pull the woman's blonde extensions from her ratty hair and claw her eyes out of her overly tanned face?"

A chuckle bubbles from my chest. "No."

"Because I didn't. Malcolm Peppernick, you make me feel like no matter how many beautiful women are around, you only see me."

I let out a long breath. "I didn't even notice her. You're..." I let the sentence go unfinished as I pull her closer until her cheek is again against my chest. For the next few moments, or minutes, or maybe hours...we stand basking in the sunlight as the shadows continue to grow more defined and the birds continue their feast. In our own world, we hold one another with a silent contentment I can't describe.

Finally, I break the serenity of the moment. "Mandy Wells, I've never met a woman like you." I lean back, again making eye contact. "When I said you were so much more than those women, I want you to know that it's my inadequate way of saying that you're amazing. I meant it when I said that I want all of you, but as long as you'll let me have this..." I kiss her forehead—my way of letting her know I love her insight, intellect, conversations, and everything about her on the inside. "...and this..." My eyebrows wiggle as I reach for the sash of her robe and begin to pull. "...I'll wait for more."

"If that's enough?"

"For now, it is..."

Before Mandy can say any more, I lean down and kiss the sensitive spot where her neck and collarbone meet. The way her flesh peppers with goose bumps and her grip of my waist tightens tells me that I have her full attention.

Slowly, I tug again on the sash until the knot is freed and the front of the robe gapes open. To my delight, I'd been correct in assuming that the robe was all she put on before coming to the balcony.

I gently guide Mandy until her back is against the rail. Once her hands are secured to the top of the rail, I fall to my knees.

"Malcolm?"

Our gazes meet for a moment as her tits heave with exaggerated breaths.

"Right now, I'm going to take what I have, take it and make you remember that I've been there. Tell me, are you all right with that?"

A moan of acknowledgment accompanies the nodding of her head. As I push her legs apart, her lips open as her eyelids, heavy with need, flutter and her hips writhe. Leaning forward I nudge my nose, lips, and chin closer to her core. "Beautiful, you smell so good."

"Malcolm..."

My name is drawn out as my tongue laps her folds and her knees quake.

Lifting one of her legs, I place it over my shoulder, opening her to my desires.

This is what I want, but this isn't about me. It's about my beautiful Mandy, showing her how damn much she means to me, how much I love...being with her. She won't allow me to say the words, but I can damn well show her.

"Oh..." Her words stutter as her grip of the railing tightens. The top of the barrier is silver, some solid metal, but the lower portion is Plexiglas, clear to the world, the bay, and the birds. We're fifteen stories in the sky, so all that would be visible from the beach would be her long dark hair as her head falls backward, her arms opened wide, and her robe.

My view is much better.

Mandy's hands slip and grip as I lick and suck, eliciting her moans and whimpers. It's as I suck her clit that her sailor talk begins, a hushed whisper until her legs begin to tremble and her words lose meaning but grow in volume. It's as I reach for her waist to hold her in place, bringing her to her cliff's edge and pushing her off to her release that she gasps for breath and springs up onto her toes. Her body quakes until the rigidity is gone and her legs go limp.

Not releasing my hold of her, I stand. She dives toward me, our lips uniting as her tongue delves deep, searching for her own taste. When our kiss ends, her light-blue eyes are open and on me.

"If that's your way of saying you're sorry, if you ever want to apologize again, I'm game."

Our bed is only a few feet away. With a smile, I reach down and scoop her into my arms.

"Malcolm!"

"Beautiful, the way your legs were shaking...I wouldn't want you to fall."

I push back the glass door and lay her on the big bed. Without a word, she eases her arms from the robe. As I lean over her, she reaches for the hem of my shirt.

Before lifting it over my head, she says with a smile, "I think I'm ordering one of these when I get home."

I look down. Upon the T-shirt in faded lettering it says BOLTZ with a lightning bolt beneath. "Or you can have this one."

"I can?"

"If you'll make me one promise."

Mandy's eyes open wide as she lifts the hem, removes it from my torso, and continues to hold it in her grasp. "What would that be?"

"That you'll wear it to bed. That I can imagine you sleeping in my shirt and nothing else."

Her cheeks rise as her smile grows. "I'll definitely wear it to bed." She lifts it to her nose. "And I love that it smells like you. I can't, however, promise the *nothing else*. You see, I don't always sleep alone. Sometimes I wake and, well, my son has found his way to my bed."

I imagine Mandy with a little *her*, a little boy *her,* and it makes me smile. "Okay...save the sleeping naked for me."

"It's a deal."

As I reach for the waistband of my shorts, Mandy does the same, covering my hand with hers and pulling my shorts down. She smiles as my cock breaks free.

"Shit," she says. "Walking may not be in the cards for today."

My grin grows. "I told you that I'd return you perhaps a little sore and worn out, but with your fantasies fulfilled. Tell me, beautiful Mandy, what fantasy have we left unfilled?"

Her upper lip disappears as her stare stays transfixed to mine. I can tell she has something in mind, but I don't know what she's thinking.

"Mandy?"

With a slight shake of her head, she scooches back farther onto the bed. Before I can say a word, she twists and comes up on her hands and knees, her sexy ass pointing my direction. It's just like at my apartment our first night—the one night. With a crook of her neck, she peers at me over her shoulder. "That thing...?"

It's fucking adorable to see her being bashful and precocious at the same time. When I said that I wanted all of her, this wasn't what I meant, but seeing her ready-and-willing pussy and ass, I swear my cock grows harder than before.

"Oh, yes." I climb onto the bed as her ass wiggles in anticipation. "Are you sure?"

"Baby steps, just like before." She nods her head. "I'm not sure about more, but what you did...I am sure. It was..." Her words trail away.

My fingers dip into her tight pussy as she writhes to my touch.

So warm and wet, her insides squeeze tighter as I add another finger. Slowly, I move in and out, each time spreading her essence, higher and higher until I reach her other opening. The tip of my finger circles her tight ring of muscles and her body quakes with the knowledge of what's coming.

"Are you sure?" I ask, teasing the barrier.

"Yes..." Her ass pushes toward me.

"Fuck!" she screams as my finger plunges beyond the barrier. Her head falls forward as she pushes back for more.

"Tell me that you want this."

"Yes, Malcolm..." Her answer is breathy as she pushes toward me. "So...good."

I can't take it anymore—I need to be inside her. With my finger still buried, I line up the tip of my cock. One hard thrust and she calls out my name, followed by a string of cuss words, as her pussy strangles my dick and her ass writhes against my finger.

"So full..." she pants.

I agree. I'm in heaven, and I never want to leave.

CHAPTER
Twenty Two

Amanda

"What are you thinking?" Sally asks as we sit under the shade of a big umbrella.

Our table is one of many on the beach. My toes continue to wiggle in the sand as we sip mimosas and enjoy the atmosphere. Malcolm and Brian told us to meet them at the seaside restaurant after our massages. I have no idea where they went or what they have planned. But I think that's how kidnappings are supposed to go. I think the kidnappee is bound to do whatever the kidnapper says. Though I'm really not well versed, I'm also not arguing.

"I feel like I'm playing make-believe," I finally answer.

Sally laughs. "I admit that this is pretty cool."

We both look out to the horizon. Just beyond the sea wall is the beautiful water. Malcolm may have said it isn't the ocean, but it's the most beautiful body of water I've ever seen. The blues are stunning as they change color from light to dark as they come together with the blue horizon. I try to imagine a sunset like he described with reds and oranges that flood the sky. I read somewhere that there's a flash of green for just a microsecond when the sun hits the water's edge. I don't know if that's true. It's not as if the sun actually makes contact with the water, but I'd love to watch and see.

I reach out to Sally's hand. "And we're both here. Doesn't it seem like a dream...like it's surreal?"

"Just remember that tomorrow we'll both be back at work, and you'll be dealing with Cruella."

I scrunch my nose and drop her hand. "Why? Why would you ruin it?"

"Because saying that isn't ruining it. It's reality, and even though this all seems too good to be true, it isn't. We're really here. This is really our reality."

"I don't know when I've been this happy...well, not *happy*. I'm happy a lot. Jase makes me happy...so does my family...and you...and maybe even my job."

"Yes, yes. You love saving puppies."

"I do. And over the years I've remembered how to laugh at movies, TV shows, and books, and how to enjoy my life again. But this is more. This doesn't feel like my life. I think the word I'm looking for is carefree. For the first time in...I can't remember how long...I feel carefree, and it scares me."

"Do me a favor."

"What?"

Sally moves her sunglasses up so she can see me clearer or maybe it's so I can see her. Either way, her hazel eyes peer from under the tinted lenses. "Enjoy it. Don't overthink it. Don't analyze it. Don't even try to understand it. Just enjoy it."

"Live in the moment?"

"Exactly."

I sigh, letting out a long breath. "That's exactly what I keep telling Malcolm that we have to do."

"Then heed your own advice. I mean, eventually you need—"

"No." I lift my hand. "Don't eventually me."

"Okay, honey, the moment." Sally takes another drink. "If I would have told you years ago when we were, like, ten and sneaking into Alec's room to snoop around that one day we'd be sitting together on some beach, drinking mimosas after a marvelous massage..." We both sigh at the memory. "...with two hot, sexy ex-jocks, you would have told me I was crazy."

"Because you are crazy. You've always been crazy."

She laughs. "It's one of my most endearing traits."

I tilt my head. "You've got a lot of great traits. I love you."

"I love you too, and I can't wait to tell your mom how happy you've been all weekend."

My brow furrows. "Is it bad that I feel guiltier if she knows?"

"You know that she wants you to have fun too, right?"

I nod, knowing she's right. Even Alec is supportive—ridiculously overprotective but supportive. Taking a long sip of my drink, I watch the way the sunlight dances on the waves.

A moment later, without any sound, or perhaps mingled with all the other sounds, I somehow know Malcolm is there. It is a shift in the air or maybe his cologne. I don't know how, but somehow the small hairs on the back of my neck stand in anticipation and I know...and then, before I can turn, his large warm hand lands gently yet possessively on my shoulder a second before he speaks.

It's a funny thing that he does, his way of needing to be connected, to touch. In the two months since our first night, I'm surprised at how accustomed I've become to it—that touch before he speaks. His deep voice brings a smile to my face.

"Hey beautiful." His lips graze my cheek.

"Hey."

Brian is giving Sally a kiss as I turn my attention to Malcolm, watching as he pulls up a chair and sits beside me.

"I know we're leaving tonight," he begins, "but while you two were getting your massages, we pulled a few strings."

My lower lip disappears behind my teeth. "Malcolm, I have to be back tonight, before late."

He shakes his head. "Our reservations for our flight are for six o'clock. That means we need to leave for the airport by four. With the time difference, you'll be home and to your son by eight."

"He goes to bed—"

Sally clears her throat. "If you don't think your mother knows Ja—"

My vigorous head shaking stops her from completing Jase's name.

She goes on, "...that your mother knows that Jay-sus himself couldn't keep you away. She also knows *his* schedule. If you don't think she does, I'm very disappointed."

Malcolm grins. "Don't you know, Sally, that I'm not allowed to know his name? And that's okay, but I know he has a great mom, and he's in bed on school nights by eight-thirty."

I reach out to Malcolm's knee. "It's not that you...it's that—"

His lips still my answer with a kiss. "Stop. You'll be home in time. I promise. But first, Brian and I secured an afternoon charter out on the bay. I can't get you to an ocean this weekend, but if we hurry to the docks, I can get you to the gulf."

"What?" Sally asks.

"Yes," Brian answers. "We called some old friends. They used to do charters all the time for the team. Apparently, they still do. When they heard that Pep and I were looking for a last-minute boat, they cancelled some poor sap's reservations..."

"No!" Sally and I say together.

"It's no big deal. Something about a fiftieth anniversary..."

"What?" Sally says, her eyes huge.

Malcolm's laugh rings over our table. "No. Brian's exaggerating. Like he always does..."

Brian innocently shrugs.

"Really," Malcolm goes on, "it's not a big boat, but it's big enough to take us out in the gulf with some wine and food and show you lovely ladies why you need to return to the sunshine state. And no one's reservations were cancelled—just the captain's day off."

"I-I..." I begin, unsure what to say.

"Let me guess," Malcolm says with a grin. "You've never been on a charter to the Gulf of Mexico before?"

My worries about Jase disappear. Though a small part of me

still feels guilty that I won't be home sooner, I know Malcolm won't let me down. He'll get me there before Jase goes to bed.

"I was going to say that since I'm the one who's kidnapped, I guess I don't have a choice." When Malcolm simply looks at me, I let my smile grow. "And I'm very excited. You're right, I've never been on a boat in any sort of saltwater before." I kiss his cheek. "Thank you!"

One of the Great Lakes is the only large body of water I'd ever seen before this weekend. A few times when Alec and I were young, our parents took us to Lake Michigan. I recall as a child thinking that it was an ocean. It's big and blue and cold, the last a contrast to this bay. Each time I've stepped into the waves here, the temperature is much warmer. There's something about the salt air, too. "I can't wait," I confess.

"Good," Malcolm says, laying a few bills on the table. "Then let's go."

I'm glad the charter comes complete with a captain and one crewman, even if we did mess up their day off. I don't doubt that Malcolm could steer a boat if he said he could. So far, I haven't found many things—anything—that he can't do. Yet it's nice to have him beside me as the boat crashes through the waves, taking us beyond the confines of Tampa Bay and out into the gulf.

While the captain drives—is that what one does with a boat? —the mate is responsible for keeping us fed while at the same time supplying us with wine and water. As plates of food continue to appear, I decide that once again, this is like nothing I've ever done. I almost wonder if it's really me sailing through the blue as the saltwater sprays in tiny droplets upon my sunglasses and we move farther and farther away from Tampa. Once we pass under a giant bridge, high above our heads, Malcolm tells me we're in the Gulf of Mexico and asks me what I think.

"Are there ever times when you can't come up with words that are sufficient to express what you're thinking?"

He smiles, not rushing me or pushing me to say more.

"It's stunning," I say, knowing my answer is woefully insufficient.

The pad of Malcolm's thumb runs over my cheek, wiping away the sea droplets. "Are you wearing sunscreen?"

"Yes, and sunglasses, and a hat when the wind doesn't blow it from my head."

"Your cheeks are the perfect pink and..." His finger drops to the edge of my beach cover-up. "I can't wait to find your tan lines." We kiss. "Mandy, you're stunning. This is water and sun. Over seventy percent of the earth is covered with water and the sun hits everywhere at some time. But you are..." His deep voice rumbles through me, surpassing the crashing waves and motor's roar. "...you are...well, there's only one of you."

"Thank goodness," Sally says, interrupting our private moment. "I love her, but the world isn't ready for two of her."

We all laugh.

As we all settle to watch the amazing view, Malcolm reaches for my hand. It's the touch, the connection, and as our fingers intertwine, I contemplate how there's only one Malcolm too.

CHAPTER
Twenty Three

Amanda

*I*s it true that for every good moment there's an equally as harsh one? I'm not sure, but as I sit across the desk from the principal at Jase's school, I feel that I may be paying my dues for the lovely weekend Malcolm and I shared only a short week and a half ago.

Sitting here is worse than any time I was ever called to the principal's office as a student. Though I did attend the same school, the principal has changed. As I sit and take in the cases of books and the windows that look out to the playground, I can't help but think that not much else is different. It's like a time machine where only the colors of paint and carpet change along with the players, yet so much stays the same. If I could, I'd willingly go back in time to be sitting here for my own transgressions, instead of hearing about my son's difficulties.

Through this all, I've come to realize that Mrs. Landecker is a caring woman and educator. Even though she is, I'd rather not have become so well acquainted with her. Unfortunately, this isn't our first encounter. I wish I could even say it was only our second. A little over two months into the school year and this is our fourth.

"Amanda," she says as I contemplate that the fact that we've gotten to a first-name basis is not necessarily a good thing. "We know," she goes on, "that you're doing all you can on your end. The thing is I'm beginning to think that Mrs. Williams and Jason aren't a good fit. That doesn't mean there's anything wrong with either one, just that there might be a better match for Jason."

She's beginning to think? Because five minutes into our second meeting, I could already have told her that. What does that mean, though?

"What options do we have?" Please don't say private school. My fingers bob against the arms of the chair as I fidget in place. "This is the school I attended, the one Jase's father and uncle attended. Are you suggesting switching schools?"

"Oh, heaven's no."

I let out a long sigh and catch my breath. Even though my lungs are operational, it doesn't help my nerves. They're still frayed beyond repair.

The first meeting, only a week or so into the year, included Mrs. Williams, Jase's teacher. An older woman, she has many times received the best-teaching award. I have no doubt that in her day the accolades may have been warranted. Now, however, she seems extremely rigid in her tried-and-true beliefs. During that meeting, the three of us spent ten minutes discussing the attributes of carpet squares and the importance of sitting still upon said square during circle time, reading time, and what seemed to amount to the better part of the day. If she'd been a salesperson, I might have ordered a lot of carpet squares right on the spot. They sounded almost magical.

"Mrs. Landecker..." I say. The first-name basis only goes one way. "...it breaks my heart that Jase is no longer excited about school. He's in kindergarten. This is supposed to be fun and exciting and ignite in him the love of learning. He told me the other day he was bad." I fight back the tears. "My son isn't bad."

Mrs. Landecker's head moves slowly back and forth as her lips form a straight line. "I agree with you. I've spoken to Jason many times. He's a sweet boy who happens to have an abundance of energy."

I pull a paper from the folder I'm holding on my lap. It's a chart with days of the week and categories, similar to the carpet-circle categories: reading, circle time, numbers, letters, raising your hand, sitting in your seat. Jase's chart has a few smiling stickers, but the majority of them are in the column entitled *working to improve*.

My hand shakes as I pass the paper toward his principal.

"Positive reinforcement..." she begins.

Once her words slow I shake my head. "This isn't positive. He's smart enough to see that others are getting more stickers than he. These charts are displayed."

"Have you ever heard of facilitative learning?"

I shake my head.

"It's not necessarily new; however, it is for our school district. It's very similar to the concept of Montessori learning. Mrs. Williams's classroom is traditional, very much like the kindergarten class you or I attended at Jason's age.

"Our district secured a grant for a pilot program. We have a new teacher in our district at our school this year, a man..."

My eyes widen: a man teaching kindergarten? I'm not sure how I feel about that.

"Amanda, I assure you Mr. P. is qualified. He came from out of state and is fully versed in the facilitative structure. With the grant, this is a multi-year program. While this is the first year of it here, the structural theory has documented support..."

My nerves seem to have calmed a bit, I realize, as I listen to her explain the theory of facilitative learning as it's applied to a classroom of small children.

She laughs, easing my mind. "I'll admit for those of us who aren't used to it, sometimes it appears more like managed chaos, but I can attest to you that the parents and students have been overly pleased.

"This theory stems from the belief that moving is related to cognitive function. Movement can enhance learning."

I want to ask how that works with children glued to carpet squares, but I don't.

"In essence," she goes on, "instead of telling students what they need to learn, in Mr. P.'s classroom, students discover learning on their own. It's that desire that helps them move freely among different activities."

I shake my head. "I don't understand. How does a kindergartener know what he needs to learn?"

"I had the same question." She pauses, studying my reaction.

"I wish I could introduce you to Mr. P. today, but his class is on a field trip. You see, kindergarten students come to us with an array of backgrounds. Many, like Jason, have attended preschool and have parents like yourself who have spent time working with them. They are familiar with a classroom setting, being around other children, and come to us with a knowledge base that years ago was meant to be accomplished by the end of this school year."

"Do you think that's the problem...that Jase is bored? Did we teach him too much?"

She shakes her head. "I'm an educator. There's never too much. However, in the traditional setting where everyone must sit and recite numbers or the alphabet, to those students who are already familiar it can seem redundant and even...yes...boring."

"How is this facilitative structure different?"

"I'll tell you what, even though Mr. P.'s class is out of the building, let me show you his classroom."

I look down at my watch. I'd told Cruella de Vil that I'd be only an hour late, but now that I'm here, and for the first time feeling hopeful, I can't stop now. "I'd love to see it."

As we enter the kindergarten hallway, the classroom Mrs. Landecker leads me to is noticeably different. Of course, there are numbers above smart boards and letters in large colorful posters throughout, but there's no line of desks. Instead there are clusters of desks and additional round tables with tubs of manipulative items: spongy letters, numbers, and shapes.

I simply stand and turn a full circle as I take in the difference. There's something in the air that's reassuring, such as a scent or a presence. I can't put my finger on it, but somehow it eases my anxiety.

"You said managed chaos?" I ask.

"Yes, you see," she explains, going to a table and lifting a lowercase letter B. She turns it one way. "It's a b," she says. Then she turns it the other way. "It's also a d."

My eyes narrow. "All right."

"Dyslexia is more common than we realized."

"Are you saying that Jase...?" I'd never noticed him reversing letters.

"No, I'm not. I'm explaining how a three-dimensional letter satisfies more senses in a child than a two-dimensional letter on a board or on a piece of paper. They can pick it up, manipulate it, and understand it."

She pulls out two other letters: a lowercase U and a lowercase G. She then places the letters on the table and spells *bug*. With a smile, she asks, "If you were Jason and you were allowed to discover on your own that if you simply..." She turns over the B...and creates the word *dug*. "...could manipulate one letter and create a whole new word, it makes learning to spell a process of discovery rather than rote memory."

"And it's more fun," I say with an understanding smile.

"It seems to be. Mr. P.'s classroom is filled with engaged learners." She takes a step toward me. "I'm not trying to pry, but without a father figure at home, Mr. P. could also be a good influence as a positive male role model for Jason."

I want to argue that Jase has my father and brother as positive male role models, but I see her point. Of course, my mind momentarily goes to Malcolm. The longer we're seeing one another, the more I find myself thinking that he too could be a positive role model.

Yet I told him that I'd never introduce him to Jase.

What would happen if I did?

"Amanda, with your permission, I'd like to transfer Jason to Mr. P.'s classroom."

"When?" I ask, again taking in the surroundings.

Even Mr. P.'s desk is different. Instead of sitting like a judge in the front of the classroom, he seems to have a long work area along one wall. That's when I notice the corner filled with books.

"Mrs. Landecker? Are children in his classroom reading?"

She tilts her head. "Reading isn't on our list of kindergarten behavioral objectives, but that's the thing with this model of learning: children discover at their own speed. Jason won't be required to read by the first grade; however, if he can construct words out of foam letters at this table, then the next obvious step is wanting to put the words together in a sentence, and then put sentences together and understand stories."

Tears fight to pool on my lids as I take in all she's saying. "Yes. I see."

Her smile grows. "If you can bring him to school again tomorrow morning, I believe having you and Jason sit down for a few minutes with Mr. P. will ease your concern and help to make the change easier."

I know in my heart that Ms. DeVoe won't be happy, but priorities are priorities. "What should I tell him?"

"Tell him that tomorrow he's going to move to Mr. P.'s class."

"Will he know who that is?"

"Oh, yes. All the students know Mr. P. and most of the moms, too," she says, the last part with the biggest grin I've seen all day.

CHAPTER
Twenty Four

Amanda

My hands continue to shake uncontrollably as I drive from work to my parents' home. Forget that, my entire body is experiencing tremors. I keep replaying the scene at the office when I arrived to work after my latest meeting with Mrs. Landecker.

As soon as I arrived, I stuck my head in Ms. DeVoe's office. "Hi. I wanted to let you know I'm here."

"Amanda, come in and shut the door."

I did as she asked, taking a seat on the other side of her desk. As I looked at my manager, I thought about Mr. P.'s desk and how his wasn't set in a position of authority like Ms. DeVoe's or even Mrs. Williams's.

"I hate to be the one to mention this," Ms. DeVoe said, "but the amount of time you're missing from work lately is becoming unacceptable."

I sat forward. "My job isn't going undone. You're aware that there have been—"

"Part of your job is being here from eight until five. Things come up. You can't simply skimp on your job to finish tasks when you're not putting in the time that's required...that's expected."

"I don't skimp. You know that I'm often here after five."

"You've also missed significant chunks of time over the last few weeks..."

"I explained that my son is having—"

"I'm not asking you to make a choice between your job and your son. I'm sure it's not easy being a single mom."

With my pulse thumping, I simply replied, "Good."

"Excuse me?"

"I said good. I'm glad you're not asking me to make a choice."

"Amanda, when you're present you do excellent work. You make a good salary and have health benefits for you and your son. You need this job."

I do, she's right, but the truth is that Jase is covered under his father's military benefits. However, I do still need this job.

"...it needs to stop, now. No more unscheduled time off."

"But tomorrow—"

Ms. DeVoe's hand went in the air, stopping me before I could explain about my meeting with the principal and how tomorrow morning I would need to take Jase to school...before I could explain that for the first time since kindergarten began, I had hope.

"No, not tomorrow," she said with a tone of ultimatum. "If you plan to continue working here, you will not miss the meetings we have scheduled for the next three days. You know that every year we hold these meetings with our health insurance provider, going over the new plans for next year and all of our employee options. The mandatory sign-up is coming November first. It's your responsibility to know the plans inside and out, and this is the time." She leaned forward. "Tell me you didn't forget."

I didn't, but I did.

Instead of answering, I said, "His school starts at nine. I can be here by ten."

"I'll see you at eight sharp tomorrow morning—and check your computer. I've sent you a list of projects that need your immediate attention."

"Ms. DeVoe—"

She'd already turned away toward her computer. At the sound of her name, her neck straightened, and she turned back to me. "Is there anything else, Ms. Wells?"

Even imagining her as Glenn Close with a big hideous smile

couldn't take away my hurt and anger. All the way from Jase's school to work I'd been encouraged and even excited. And in a matter of minutes with my manager, my entire world was caving in.

As I left her office, I knew what I would do...what I would do again. I'd ask my mom to take my place. I hated that. I knew she would, but she shouldn't have to. Of course, I thought of Jackson.

If only...

And then my mind somehow went to Malcolm. I could never ask him. He has his own job, his own career. Even if things were different...it wouldn't be his responsibility to help Jase's transition at school.

Throughout the day I gritted my teeth and tried to remember puppies. I tried to remember Mr. P.'s classroom...and by gosh, I did everything—every damn thing—on Cruella de Vil's list and everything else she came up with, including adding plant-feeding sticks to her precious plants.

Apparently, Phil is still having some erection issues and she hopes the vitamin sticks will help.

Now that I am on my way to pick up Jase at my parents', I'm once again upset. I've already called Mom and of course she said yes, but that doesn't ease my anger at the unfairness.

As I pull into my parents' driveway, I see Jase in the garage with my dad. The large door is open and they're over by my dad's workbench. Getting out of my car, I start walking their direction when Jase turns. With a big smile on his face, he runs toward me, and small arms encircle my waist.

"Mom, you can't look."

"I can't? At what?"

"Grandpa and I are making you something special. It's a surprise."

I look over at my dad. He's shaking his head with a big smile.

"Thanks, Dad. You know how I *love* surprises."

"This one you will. Go see your mom." He waves me toward the house. "Us men are busy."

"Yep, us men," Jase repeats.

I give each man a kiss on the cheek and head inside.

"Oh, Amanda," my mom says as soon as she hears me enter.

Their house smells heavenly of whatever she's cooking for dinner. Why does someone else's cooking always smell so marvelous?

"What's the matter?" I ask.

"Come, let's sit down."

It's never a good sign when my mom wants to sit. So many things can be said standing. It's only the important or possibly upsetting things that require sitting. "Is it you or Dad? How about Alec? Is everyone all right?"

"No, dear, it's nothing like that," she says as she walks to the table with two cups of tea. "Here, it's getting cold out there. Warm tea always makes things better."

"Mom, is this about tomorrow?"

"Kind of."

"Are you unable to go with him?" I hear the panic in my own tone. To hell with my job. If my mom can't go, I will. Let the chips fall where they may.

"Of course I can go to Jase's school. I just wanted to show you a note from Mrs. Williams. It was addressed to you. I'm sorry I opened it, but after your call and what you said about your meeting with the principal, I thought...well, the truth is I was curious."

I slowly reach for the envelope. That's another bad sign. A note that says *Hey, your child is doing great* doesn't come in an envelope. I remove the page of paper and begin to read.

Mrs. Harrison,

I look up. "I've told that woman a hundred times my name is Wells."

"Some people have difficulty with that."

"Obviously," I say before I go back to reading.

Mrs. Harrison,

Today was a particularly trying day with Jason. Though he obviously knows the material, he refused to participate in class, saying he was tired. I sent him to the nurse's office, but after a few minutes he returned. During rest time, he was no longer tired, but rambunctious.

In my experience, I have seen this situation helped with a doctor's intervention.

I will be sending a recommendation in the next day. Please consider this option for the future success of Jason's educational experience.

Mrs. Williams

"What?" I ask. "She thinks he needs a doctor. Why?"

"I can only assume to settle him down."

"No."

My mom reaches out, and her hand covers mine. "Honey, I don't think it's out of the question. It's very helpful for some children. However, I think she didn't know yet about the class change. In my opinion, this class change may be the best thing for Jase. You can keep the possibility of seeing a doctor in mind if the change in classrooms doesn't work, but didn't you say this other teacher has a different strategy?"

I lean my forehead down to the table. My voice is muffled. "Mom, this is so hard."

She touches my hair. "No one said parenting was easy."

I look back up. "But it's not supposed to be done alone..."

"You're not alone. I'm here. Your dad is here. And what about Malcolm, that man you've been seeing?"

As opposed to another Malcolm?

I don't even answer. She knows how I feel about that. Instead, I focus on the new classroom. "Mrs. Landecker said the new classroom is organized- or managed-chaos, but it works. Did I tell you the teacher is a man?"

Mom leans back against the kitchen chair and smiles. It's

closed lip, like she does when she's contemplating. "That might be just what the doctor ordered."

I shake my head. "I don't think that's what Mrs. Williams had in mind."

Mom looks toward the door that leads to the garage, making sure we're alone. "That woman's an old biddy with antiquated notions. She needs to retire. I like what Mrs. Landecker has in mind. It certainly can't hurt to try."

I finally reach for my tea. "I hope so."

"Will you and Jase stay for dinner? I made plenty."

"Does he have any homework?" It's silly to me that kindergarteners have homework, but he does.

"It's all done. That's how I found the note."

"I have food at home to cook."

"And I have food here that's already cooked," she says with a bigger grin.

"Thanks, Mom."

CHAPTER
Twenty Five

Malcolm

I can't take my eyes off of Mandy. She's gorgeous and so fucking fuckable. The way the brown waves of her silky hair spill over my pillow and her bruised lips lift to a sexy-as-hell smile makes me perpetually hard. Having her ride my dick in the front seat of her car was exhilarating, but that's not the kind of woman she is.

Mandy Wells is a thousand-count Egyptian sheets, brass bed, and soft piped-in music kind of woman. She's the best life has to offer...She's champagne and caviar.

Maybe champagne and pizza. Okay, wine and pizza. Fine, wine and great pizza.

That's okay. I prefer her that way.

Since we've been seeing each other, each time together is something new. Mandy is spontaneous, sexy, and responsive as hell. She's also responsible and caring. She's all of those things wrapped into one beautiful package. Whether she's thinking about her responsibilities or enjoying an outing on the Gulf of Mexico, she's everything I never knew I wanted.

As her eyes close and her smile rests, I crawl over her luscious body, covering it with mine. Even with the outside temperature dropping, she doesn't need blankets—I'll be her blanket. My cock twitches as it grows and rubs against her thighs.

Her gorgeous blue eyes open. "Malcolm, umm, didn't we just do that?"

"Didn't I just fuck you until you screamed every cuss word I've ever heard?"

Her cheeks rise. "I bet you've heard others."

"Nope. And I spent six years in a locker room. That is very impressive, Ms. Wells."

"I think you're exaggerating..."

Her words trail away as the tip of my hard cock teases her folds and her legs slowly part. She is right. We did just do this, but damn, with her beside me, I'm hard again.

I know there's been things happening with her son, things that have been worrying her, but as of yet, she hasn't trusted me with that side of her life. I understand. I'll take what I can get. Right now, Mandy's in my bed and I want to be inside her, buried in her wet, warm heaven. I want to make her forget whatever else in this world is bothering her.

"Happy anniversary," I whisper as I sink deep inside her.

She stutters as her back arches and her lips form that adorable 'O.' "W-what anniversary?"

"We met three months ago, today."

I bask in her smile as she wiggles and moves with my rhythm.

During those three months, we've stolen moments to be together whenever we could. Only that one time did I have her for an entire weekend. I've been racking my brain for ideas on how to do it again.

I long for nights like this when she can be in my bed, when we have more than an hour here or two there. I'm addicted to her presence, not only in my bed, but in my life. I long to have her on the sidelines when my team plays soccer, beside me at school functions...beside me in life. I fantasize about flying her to Florida again, but this time to meet my parents and catch another Lightning game.

I've never known a woman like Mandy—Amanda—before. I've never wanted to spend my time with the same woman, yet I miss her every second we're apart. She's my drug and I'm addicted, enthralled by her zeal for life.

Her fingernails bite into the skin of my back as I pump harder.

The way her pussy hugs my dick is also addicting. I tell myself we'll only go out to dinner, to the movies, or for drinks. Mandy agrees, and then...

We find ourselves connected, me inside her, her surrounding me, her gorgeous tits in my face, and her essence covering my fingers, tongue, and cock. Thank goodness she finally told me she was on birth control and we agreed to be as close as possible. The way she said it, it almost seemed like a new development, but how could a woman like Mandy not be on birth control?

Our world shakes as her entire body stiffens. I open my eyes.

It's one of my favorite views, watching her come. I love the way for a moment everything else in the world disappears, and she enjoys the pleasure inside her.

I kiss her nose. "You're amazing."

Mandy shakes her head. "I think that's you."

Though I don't want to, I ease out of her. "I wish you'd stay all night."

"My son is spending the night with my parents, but I need to be there in the morning."

I reach for her hand. "What happened to his dad?"

The happiness of a moment ago is gone. I haven't pushed, but it's been three months and I want to know.

"Malcolm..."

"Beautiful, I'm not going anywhere. There's nothing you can say that will scare me away."

Her lips disappear between her teeth, one by one, as she contemplates telling me her story. I pull her close, her cheek to my chest, and wait. With the comfort of the soft sheet and blanket over our bodies, we lie in the stillness for what seems like an eternity. Only the sound of our breathing and the light hum of the furnace warming the apartment fill the air.

I have ideas about what could have happened to her son's father. Maybe he's a jerk and didn't want kids. Maybe he's in prison. What I didn't anticipate was the reality.

Mandy speaks quietly, replacing the rhythm of our breaths with the awful truth. "He was killed by an IED."

I feel like a jerk with the scenarios I'd imagined. None of them had included her being a widow. Then again, what she just said makes sense. I couldn't imagine any man willingly leaving this beautiful woman, not her and not a kid. As her shoulders shudder, I kiss the top of her head, tasting the hair spray and shampoo. "I'm sorry. Thank you for telling me."

I pull her tighter as her pain—her loss—emanates from her every pore. It's a dense cloud surrounding us. It's not pretty. But life isn't always pretty. This is the truth I want to share, the reality I want to navigate beside her, if she'll allow me.

After another long pause, she speaks again, "You're the first...the only...other than him. I know we started this sex thing fast, but I hadn't...not in five years."

I run my hand over her hair, smoothing the waves and wanting her to know how much I care for her. Hell, it's more than care. Over the past three months I've fallen in love with her. I hug her tighter. "So the birth control?"

"I never needed it."

"I never thought you slept around."

She lifts her tearstained cheeks. "Really? We did it in the front seat of my car on our second date."

My grin broadens. "We did and in my apartment the first night we met. I'll never forget either time. You were fantastic. I love it when you ride my cock."

"You do?"

The way she asks brings my body back to life one more time. "I do. I love the way your tits bounce in my face and the way your knees squeeze my hips."

Mandy shakes her head as she pushes herself up. "You know I'm tired, right?"

"I know you love to ride my cock as much as I love having you do it."

"Fuck," she mumbles as she moves and straddles my hips.

"No, beautiful. You're supposed to save the cussing for when you come apart."

"Because you're confident enough to think you can make me do that for a third time tonight?"

I reach down and position my now-hard-again dick at her pussy. Before entering, I say, "No, not confident—cocky enough."

"Yes, Mr. Peppernick, you are cock—"

My dick interrupts her smart remark as it slides into its favorite place on earth.

"Oh fuck!" she gasps as her neck stretches and her tits fill my vision.

With her hands on my shoulders and tits in my face, Mandy moves up and down, slow at first, adjusting and accommodating. Her pussy is like a glove—two sizes too small—that fits perfectly around me. It may seem like the timing sucks, but in reality, it feels like part of the process, her process. Her moving through the cloud of hurt and sorrow, maybe for once accepting that she doesn't have to do it alone.

There's something about this time, slow, with her in total control, that seems to satisfy her in a way words can't. I want Mandy to know she's safe with me, her stories and her heart. We can take it slow or fast, whatever she wants.

When we finally settle again, I kiss her hair. "I'm sorry."

"I don't think sorry is what you meant. You meant, *damn, Mandy, that was great*."

I scoff. "Yes, it was. I'm sorry about your son's dad."

"My husband..." she clarifies before going on. "We were married for only two years, but we were together forever. He was my brother's best friend. From the time we were all little kids, he was always around..."

In my darkened bedroom, we lie awake for hours as she talks. For three months I couldn't get her to tell me anything, and in one night I'm hearing it all. Her life, words, and emotions are fully on display. In many ways, she's more exposed than she was that first night. Story after story comes forth, one ending as another begins. With each one, Mandy lets me into her life and her heart; though her son is mentioned, it's her husband's name I learn. Through it all I hear how much she loved Jackson, how they loved one another. Theirs was something special. It was that once-in-a-lifetime attraction that's meant to be forever. My heart breaks as she recalls him leaving after their son's birth, his promise to return, and the fateful knock on her door. While it hurts to hear her pain, I like that she doesn't hold back.

My chest stays perpetually damp with her tears.

When she finally stops talking, her breathing stills, and I can tell she's fallen asleep.

I don't care that she wants to go home. I'm not letting her go tonight. I never want to let her go. Instead, I hold her tightly as she sleeps.

It's strange as I contemplate all she told me.

I never imagined falling for someone, falling in love with someone, and then holding that someone while she possibly dreamt of someone else, but for some reason, it feels right.

I'm honored that Mandy finally let me in—trusted me—not just into her body, but also with a glimpse into her heart. Knowing her story helps me to understand her trepidation. It makes sense. But as I lie with her in my arms, I wish I could make her understand that I'll never try to replace Jackson. What they had together shouldn't be replaced. What I'd like to do is love her too. She deserves that.

As I fall asleep, I hope that someday she'll decide there's room in her heart and her life for me too.

CHAPTER

Amanda

The coffee shop is packed with Black Friday shoppers as Sally and I sit at a small table, surrounded by our bounty. We've been shopping since late Thanksgiving night and now the sun is once again up. While the sales aren't all they used to be, and normally online shopping is my favorite option—it's convenient and I can do it late at night in my pajamas—shopping on Black Friday is our tradition. We've done it ever since we were young, going out to the stores with our moms. Sally's mom and dad have moved to Florida for the colder months. Snowbirds is what they're called and they love every moment. The last few years, when it comes to fighting the crowds, my mom has chosen to stay home with Jase and Dad and decorate the house for Christmas. Therefore, that leaves just Sally and me, and neither one of us would miss it for the world.

"I think you've about got the Santa thing covered," Sally says, inspecting my bags.

"With this and what's already in the trunk of the car, I think you might be right." I shrug. "Besides, Monday is Black Monday and with Amazon Prime, I'll get whatever I missed."

"Don't remind me. Last year I dropped a fortune, and I don't even have a son."

"No, but you're Aunt Sally and you always do too much."

She smiles over the rim of her coffee. "It's not all for Jase. I still enjoy shopping for myself."

I peek at the bags near her boots. "I noticed."

"Hey, I can take some of your stuff to my place if you want and keep it hidden."

"That would be great..."

We go on to discuss the fun of hiding the presents and what we remember when we were the little ones waking on Christmas morning. It's hard not to think about Jackson when Jase is so excited. But every year, I've worked to make our private Christmas as special as it would be if Jackson could be there. Then, after our private presents and pancakes, we head over to my parents' house for round two and finally to Jackson's parents' place for round three.

Though his parents aren't as involved as mine, they're always excited to spend time with Jase.

"What's Malcolm doing this long weekend?" Sally asks.

"He went to visit his parents. Oh! They live in Florida too."

"And he didn't think we should have met them while we were there?"

I just shake my head. "Too real, thank you."

"Well, I'm not surprised that they live there. Just think, he'll come back all tan." Her eyebrows do a little dance. "Tan-line discovery."

"I never told you—"

"What? Spill. He's amazing in bed and all you want for Christmas is a great big O?"

I giggle. "Subject is off-limits. I've told you that."

"I've told you about Brian. He's—"

"See," I interrupt, shaking my head. "The thing is that I don't want to know."

"The best...that's all I was going to say. I know how you are. No sexy details for my former-nun best friend."

I laugh at that. "Former?"

"Yep. Whenever you mention Pep, you're all giddy and shit. I think the only praying you're doing now is calling out to God during those O's."

"You're awful and possibly sacrilegious."

"Wait, what were you going to tell me? What haven't you told me? We're best friends. I'm supposed to know everything."

It's then I remember the change in Jase. "This isn't what I was going to tell you, but let me just say that since they moved Jase to that new teacher, it's been the difference of night and day. He loves everything about his new class. It's exactly what I was praying and hoping for..." *Between my search for O's.* "...and the teacher...Jase is all 'Mr. P. said' or 'Mr. P. did'..."

"And you still haven't met this famous and mysterious Mr. P.?"

I shake my head as I take a sip of my coffee. "No. I mean, I doubt he's very mysterious. It's just that Cruella de Vil has been especially bitchy. Mom met him the first day Jase went to his classroom. She said he was nice and handsome..." I mimic my mother's voice. "...and he wasn't wearing a wedding ring."

Sally laughs. "Your mom's hilarious."

"It's not just Mr. P. Now that she knows Malcolm's name—thanks to you and my kidnapping—she mentions often that maybe it would be good for Jase and Malcolm to meet..." I shake my head as I take another drink. "Besides, as far as Mr. P. goes, Jase's principal said that he's a new teacher, so I figure he's what...twenty-two or twenty-three?"

"Girl, you're twenty-five. A younger man might be fun."

"Almost twenty-six and no thanks. Mommy to one little boy is enough. Besides, I'm kind of seeing Malcolm." *And he's a man, not a boy.* I don't say that, but the thought makes my insides pinch in just the right way.

"Kind of?" Sally asks. "Yes, you kind of have been seeing one another, for what...over three months?"

"Yes," I agree. "We just celebrated our three-month anniversary."

"I thought only high school students did that shit. Next you're going to tell me you've been doodling his name with yours at work on your ink blotter." Her voice goes up an octave. "Malcolm plus Amanda..."

"It wasn't as if we actually celebrated. The night was...emotional."

Sally's smile fades. "Emotional? Why? What's the matter?"

"This is what I haven't told you..."

"Oh, honey...did he break it off? Did you? Why?"

"No," I say. "That's not it. I told him about Jackson."

My best friend's hazel eyes open wide as they fill with unshed tears. "You what?"

I simply nod, holding back my own tears. "I told Malcolm all about Jackson. He listened. He didn't question or act jealous. He just held me and made me feel safe, like it was all right to share and grieve and be honest. After I poured out my heart, I fell asleep in his arms, listening to his heartbeat, feeling drained yet somehow lighter."

Sally's tears are no longer confined to her eyes. They're now streaming down her face. Wiping them away, she mutters, "Damn sleep deprivation. I need a fucking nap."

"Yeah, apparently, I was sleep-deprived that night too, because I cried through the whole thing."

"And now?"

I shrug. "In a way, it doesn't change anything: Jackson is still gone. I'm still Jase's only parent, yet at the same time, as I said, it feels different. Lighter somehow. I don't even know how to explain it."

"Girl, Malcolm is the whole package."

My grin returns. "No, remember, he is just one night."

"Oh, that's right." She lifts her paper cup of coffee and offers a caffeine-infused toast. "To one fucking long night...like maybe one that lasts the next fifty years."

We clink cups. Not really. Paper doesn't make a sound.

"I'm scared to think of forever."

"Then just keep it to one night. No one is rushing you. Keep it one night and maybe tomorrow time will stand still. What about introducing Jase?"

I shake my head. "I'm not ready to bring them together yet. Besides, with Mr. P. in Jase's life, I don't think Malcolm could compete."

"It's not a competition."

"Maybe for the first time in years, time isn't my enemy. Maybe we have time for that in the future. Like...way in the future."

Sally looks down at the screen of her phone. "No, time's not an enemy with your handsome men, but if we're going to make the early-bird specials at Pink, we need to hustle."

"I don't think Jase needs lingerie for Christmas."

Her eyebrows do the dancing thing again. "This is mommy-shopping and maybe even Pep-shopping."

"You think Malcolm needs some silky lingerie?"

"I think he wouldn't mind if you had some. Girl, when I packed for you for Florida, I noted that your supply was seriously lacking."

"Because I have so much opportunity..."

"That one silk nightgown was all I could find."

As we gather our bags, I look at Sally and grin. "Oh, was there a nightgown packed? I guess I didn't notice."

"Yes, the nun has left the building."

CHAPTER
Twenty Seven

Amanda

Snow is beginning to fall as I pull my car into the elementary school's parking lot. Though I should be thinking about the condition of the roads, my thoughts are consumed with the letter in my purse, the one telling me to be here for a meeting with Jase's new teacher. The sense of dread that I've had since I first read the note intensifies with each passing second. It bubbles through me with that paralyzing type of fear that makes moving difficult. It takes all my concentration to reach for the key and turn off the engine of my car.

For not the first time, I wish I weren't alone. I could have asked my mother. She would have come, but that's not the same.

I long for Jackson...and now, Malcolm.

That's happening more and more, and while I'm doing what Mom and Sally wanted—I'm living—a part of me feels guilty that I think of Malcolm in that way. I would never try to replace Jackson, but as Sally and Mom have been telling me, life goes on.

I know I should have shared with Malcolm more about Jase and his issues at school; after all, he's a teacher and a coach. He's familiar with kids, but I'd assume he's used to older ones. Now that he talks about his hockey days, he's told me how he used to volunteer with a U12 hockey league in Florida.

Five-year-old boys are not the same as ten- and eleven-year-old boys. The honest truth is that the more attracted I become to Malcolm, the more afraid I am of letting Jase get close. There's nothing holding Malcolm to me. What if he doesn't want the drama of a kindergarten boy?

He could leave.

That's what could happen.

And what if Jase becomes as attached to Malcolm as I have? Malcolm's leaving would be devastating to both of us. I can't be the cause of any more disappointment for Jase.

I say it's because of Jase, but I know it's also because of me. As I contemplate the possibility of a future, it all frightens me. I'm scared to be happy. I'm scared to bring all the separate parts of my life together because if I do, it could all implode. Or worse, it could be perfect and then it could disappear.

For some reason, I remember what Alec said to me at his softball game, and I decide that it's not a lack of faith. It's fear. I'm afraid to have faith.

A tear falls down my cheek as I push those thoughts away. I don't have time for this. At this moment, I need to concentrate on the reason I'm at Jase's school. I need to focus on this upcoming meeting.

Mr. P. wants to talk with me. What if he tells me that Jase isn't a good fit for his class, that this isn't working? This kind of teaching that he's doing is a pilot program. I'm sure they don't want any failures. Yet from my perspective, I didn't think things were failing. I thought things had improved. I know that without a doubt Jase's attitude has. Even as recently as this morning, he was excited to go to school.

I look through the foggy windows at the snow. Soon it will be Christmas break. I'm afraid Mr. P. is going to recommend a private school or something else. I'm afraid I'll be spending Jase's break shopping for a new school or worse, making a doctor's appointment for him. I don't even know for sure what I'm afraid of, but I know I am.

For not the first time, I'm scared and alone.

With my car parked and a million thoughts running through my mind, I come to the realization that I'm tired of being scared. Of all the things I have to fear, faith in Malcolm shouldn't be one of them. From the moment we met, I sensed something sincere about Malcolm. Never in over three months has he given me any reason to doubt him.

Maybe I can't guarantee that Malcolm will be in Jase's life forever. I know I can't. I've learned the hard way that nothing is guaranteed. What I can do is what Alec mentioned. I can have faith in my judgment that Malcolm is a good man. Faith that the time Jase has Malcolm in his life will be positive.

Taking a ragged breath, I begin to type Malcolm a text. I know he's at work and won't get it until later, but I need to write it.

I want to write it.

Sorry to bother you at work. I should have told you, but I was afraid. I'm at my son's school for a meeting with his new teacher. I'm scared, and I wish you were here. My hand trembles as I write the part my heart tells me to write. *He's a great kid. You're an amazing man. If you'd...* I backspace to *man. Can I introduce the two of you? I would love for you two to meet.*

My heart is beating a million miles a minute. It's telling me that this is something I should have done a while ago, but still it feels a little like jumping off a cliff.

I don't expect Malcolm to take on the responsibility of Jase. I guess I just hope he'll be willing to support me as I shoulder the responsibility.

Taking a deep breath, I bend my knees and jump.

In a more literal sense, I hit send.

As I do, the alarm on my phone rings, and I read my screen.

School meeting with Jase's teacher.

I take another breath, wipe the tears from my cheeks, and do my best to pull myself together. Step by step, I keep going until I've entered the school.

"Mrs. Harrison?" the receptionist asks as she pushes the button that opens the door, allowing me to enter the school.

I shake my head. "Ms. Wells. I'm Jason Harrison's mother. I'm here for a meeting." Why is that so damn hard? I'm not the first mother in the history of time to have a different last name.

A moment later, I'm in the main office. "Yes, Ms. Wells," the older receptionist says. "Mr. P. is waiting for you in the conference room."

I follow closely behind as she leads the way to the back of the office and beyond to a hallway of conference rooms. As we approach, the ring of Jase's laughter reaches me. Suddenly, my dread and fear bubble to the surface. With my stomach in knots, I reach for the receptionist's arm. There's panic in my tone. "Is my son in there?"

"Yes," she says with a smile. "I believe he is."

"Why? If there's a problem, he's too young—"

"Ma'am, I don't think there's a problem. Mr. P.—"

We turn the corner and two sets of blue eyes turn our direction. The ones I love and have since the day he was born and laid in my arms, and the other, the sexiest, most stunning blue eyes I know. That second pair renders me mute, staring at me with obvious shock. My feet forget to move as his gaze holds me captive.

"Ms. Wells is here," the receptionist says.

Malcolm stands, confusion evident on his face. "Wells? Harrison?"

"Yes, I'm sorry," the older woman says. "I had it wrong. Ms. Wells is Jason Harrison's mother."

Jase jumps from the chair beside Malcolm and runs toward me. "Mommy, this is Mr. P. He says I'm doing good!" His sweet voice rings through the conference room.

"Good?" I can hardly speak as tears fill my eyes. It's difficult to pull my gaze from Malcolm's.

Jase grabs my hand and drags me forward. "He says we get to tell you."

Malcolm still hasn't said more than my name.

I look around. The receptionist is gone, leaving the three of us alone.

"Mr. P.?" I ask.

Malcolm's grin overtakes his expression of confusion as he shrugs. "Peppernick is hard for kindergarteners to say."

I shake my head. "I knew you were a teacher, but you never said that you taught kindergarten."

"I tried, but we agreed to keep everything centered on us—live in the moment."

"B-but you're Jase's teacher? You're *my son's* teacher."

Malcolm's smile broadens. "And you're Jason's mother. You have a marvelous son."

The weight of the world lifts off my shoulders and my heart. I blink away the tears of relief. "I do."

Malcolm lowers himself to one knee and looks at Jase. "And you, Jason, have a great mom."

Jase's smile fills his entire face. "I do." He turns to me. "See, Mom. I told you Mr. P. is cool."

"Yes, Jase. Mr. P. is very cool." I turn to Malcolm. "And this meeting isn't to say there are problems?"

Malcolm shakes his head. "No, I'm sorry if my note scared you. I thought you'd realized how well he's been doing." Malcolm pulls out a chair for me at the large table. "Jason—"

"His name is Jason," I say, interrupting. "But we call him Jase."

Malcolm turns toward Jase. "Which name do you like better?"

I'm speechless, and my chest clenches as Malcolm asks for Jase's preference.

Jase shrugs. "I like Jase best. Mrs. Williams called me Jason, and it felt mean."

Malcolm nods. "Then Jase it is." He turns back to me. "As I was saying, Jase is doing exceptionally well. He gets along with his classmates and is often the first to pick a learning center..."

I stare as Malcolm speaks, his deep voice washing away the fears and worries, and his blue eyes sparkling as if he's walking a tightrope between Jase's Mr. P. and my Malcolm. I remember the

Gulf of Mexico when we were on the boat and Malcolm asked me what I thought. I remember asking him if there were ever times when words seemed insufficient. As he continues speaking and Jase's little eyes watch with wonder and awe, I know that's what I feel. I can't describe it, but it's overwhelming.

"...already reading. We wanted to show you."

"Reading?" I ask.

"Yes."

"Mom, can I show you?"

Still unsure how to verbalize, I nod and smile as Jase climbs onto my lap with a book in his hand. His soft hair under my nose smells of little boy, and I give his head a quick kiss as he settles.

"Mom, this is one of the Christmas surprises I have for you. The other one is at Grandma and Grandpa's house."

"I remember. You made it with Grandpa."

Malcolm continues to stare at the two of us as Jase opens the book and begins to read. Each word is deliberate and precise. A few words Jase sounds out, taking time to make sure he's right, and before long he says, "The end."

I swallow back my emotions and give him a kiss on the forehead. "Baby, that was the best surprise ever."

Malcolm shares a wink that only I can see. "See?" he whispers. "Surprises can be good."

"I'm not a baby," Jase says, concentrating on me.

"No, you're not."

"What happens now, Mom, after *The end?*"

My questioning gaze goes to Malcolm. I don't know the answer. "What happens?"

"Jase, something tells me this isn't the end, but just the beginning. But I'd like to ask what your mom thinks."

I honestly don't know what I think. It's all so much. "I-I..." I take a deep breath and peer at the two sets of blue. "I think I'd like that very much."

"Then, Jase, you heard your mom. This is just the beginning."

CHAPTER

Malcolm
The Beginning

*A*fter our surprise meeting at school nearly three weeks ago, Mandy left with Jase.

I couldn't wrap my mind around what had happened until I went back to my classroom, found my phone, and read her text. For a grown man, I couldn't keep the moisture from blurring her words.

Sorry to bother you at work. I should have told you, but I was afraid. I'm at my son's school for a meeting with his new teacher. I'm scared, and I wish you were here. He's a great kid. You're an amazing man. Can I introduce the two of you? I would love for you two to meet.

Her fear and bravery come through louder than her words. I want nothing more than to hold her in my arms. It may have been fate that brought me to this town, Mandy into my life, and Jase into my classroom, but this was more. This was Mandy's invitation—what I'd been hoping for—and it came before her two worlds collided.

I texted back: *He is a great kid. You're an amazing woman, and I'm ready for the beginning.*

---

*C*hristmas music fills the air, playing from the speakers high above the zoo's attractions. Though the snow has been cleared from the sidewalks, the areas that during the summer contain flowers as well as the trees and bushes are all covered with a coating of white. Lights of all colors create a magical scene as the three of us move with the other families through the holiday displays.

Families.

I turn as Jase's mitten-covered hand fits perfectly in mine. The first thought running through my mind is that this is real. I'm really here with Mandy and Jase. I never imagined wanting a premade family while at the same time, I've never wanted anything more.

"Look, Mr. P.—I mean, Malcolm," Jase says with a shy grin as he tilts his head toward the polar bear exhibit.

Before doing as Jase says and looking at the bears, I gaze over at Mandy. As our eyes meet, her cheeks rise, making her blue eyes shine. We both know that it's an adjustment to start calling your teacher by his first name. Jase is finally getting the hang of it. The question will be if he can remember to go back to Mr. P. once school begins again in the new year.

"Let's go see them," I say, tugging Jase toward the crowd near the rail.

"You two go ahead. I'll stay back here," Mandy says as she releases Jase's other hand.

"Are you sure?" I ask.

"Yeah, I'm sure."

There aren't words to express what it means to me that she trusts me with her son, even in a crowd at a zoo. With Jase in tow, I wiggle through the people until we reach the Plexiglas rail separating us from a large cavernous ravine. On the other side of the chasm, one large polar bear paces back and forth, eyeing the crowd, as another large bear and a small cub play in what has to be freezing cold water. Having a polar bear cub born in the zoo has been a recent claim to fame for this city.

Jase looks from the bears to me and back. "Why is the one bear walking back and forth? Is he mad?"

"I think that's the dad bear. He's probably not mad, just unsure of all the people. He's protecting the mom and baby."

Jase continues to stare at the bears. Finally, he turns toward me. His voice is so low I almost can't hear him over the music and other people. "My dad died protecting us. That's what Mom says."

With a lump growing in my throat, I nod. "Your mom told me the same thing. That makes your dad a hero."

It's Jase's turn to nod. "Yep. But don't say anything to Mom. It makes her sad to talk about him."

"You can always talk about him. It's a good thing."

"Do you think I might ever get a new dad?"

"I think that's up to your mom. How would you feel about that?"

Jase's lips come together as if he's giving the topic some genuine thought. "I think it would be cool. And you know what?"

"What?"

"She's not sad when you're here, Mr. P." He shakes his head. "Malcolm."

"That's good," I say as I ruffle his hair. "I like seeing your mom happy."

"Me too."

Neither Mandy nor I were sure how Jase would feel about his teacher dating his mom, but since the first time she invited me to their apartment and the three of us went out for pizza, he's been our biggest supporter. Granted, with him along, our first night as a threesome was considerably different than Mandy's and my one night over four months ago. With the three of us, there was no starving or rehydration. My eating was limited to pizza and breadsticks.

Though Jase may be our biggest advocate, he isn't alone. Mandy's parents have been fantastic. They truly are a great support system for her. Her mother just laughed when she found out that the Malcolm Mandy has been seeing and Mr. P. are one and the same. It made our introduction easier since I'd already met her mother the first day Jase entered my classroom.

My parents too are happy. They weren't as thrilled when I told them I wouldn't make it to Florida for Christmas, but I promised I'd make it down before school begins again in January. If things go as I hope, when I do I won't be alone.

"What were you two talking about?" Mandy asks as we make our way back to her. She's all bundled in her winter coat, hat, and gloves, and even with Jase's hand in mine, I'm awestruck by her presence. The crisp air is giving her cheeks the rosy glow that's usually reserved for her cute blush.

"Polar bears," I answer as if I haven't just received the permission I've been seeking.

I know I should ask Mandy's father, and I will, but it was Jase's blessing that I sought the most. I hadn't been sure how to approach the subject. It just so happened he did it for me.

"We need to get home...it's getting late," Mandy says, reaching for Jase's other hand.

"Will you come too?" Jase asks, looking my way.

My grin grows. "I'd love to come to your place...and at it," I add softly. "But that's up to your mom."

Mandy shakes her head. "To, yes."

We both laugh, confident by Jase's expression that our joke is strictly between us and that he missed our meaning.

Three days later on Christmas Eve, I'm again at Mandy's apartment. Jase is finally asleep, after coming out to the living room nearly a half-dozen times for a variety of reasons—everything from needing a drink to having to go to the bathroom and the important news he forgot to share with us that was so important he couldn't remember it.

Now that he's asleep, I'm helping Mandy unload the gifts from the trunk of her car. They've all been wrapped, so it's more of a job of placing them under the tree than anything else.

"I can't wait to see his face when he wakes up," Mandy says as the last gift is placed, and she rehangs his filled stocking.

"There's a reason they have the saying 'like a kid on Christmas morning.'"

"Would you like a beer?" she asks once all the gifts are in place.

"I can help."

She waves me away and walks to the kitchen. As she does, I slip my surprise from my pocket into the stocking that says *Mom*. With the room's normal illumination off, the colorful tree lights create vibrant globes that reflect around the walls and on the shiny wood floor. After I sit back down, she returns.

"Here," she says, handing me a bottle as she holds tightly to the stem of a wine glass.

Before she sits, I ask, "What about your stocking?"

Mandy shrugs. "I guess I wasn't good."

"Oh, beautiful, I think you've been very good."

"Well, apparently, Santa doesn't."

"Are you sure?"

She laughs. "Since it's empty, I'd say I'm sure."

As she starts to sit, I stop her. "Why don't you make sure?"

Her blue eyes grow wide as she places the wine on the table and slowly makes her way to her stocking. "Malcolm, what did you do?"

Time stands still as she reaches into it, her fingers grasping for anything. It's as she feels what's inside that she turns my direction. The smile from earlier is gone, and her eyes are glassy with unshed tears.

"Malcolm?"

I'm not sure if this is a good reaction or not, but I've made the move so I can't turn back now. Placing my beer next to Mandy's wine, I slip from the couch to one knee, at her feet.

"Mandy, I had this all planned. I knew exactly what I was going to say, and now..." I reach for her hand, now holding the diamond ring. "...I'm reminded of the time we were on the gulf and you said words couldn't describe what you were thinking. I'm going to give it a try, but I know it won't be enough."

Her lips disappear behind her teeth as she stares down at me. The tears have now escaped, trailing down her cheeks.

I reach up and wipe one away with my thumb.

"One night with you wasn't enough. You're the fiercest, strongest, most beautiful woman I've ever met. I've been mesmerized by our attraction since our first date. When we're together, it's as if I need to touch you to be sure you're real. When we're apart, you're in my thoughts. I've known for a long time that it was love, but I respected your wishes and never talked about what I was feeling.

"I can't do that any longer. Mandy Wells, I love you. I love all of you...that means Jase too. I've tried to show it, but I want more. I want to say it. From the first day Jase walked into my classroom I knew he was special. I had no idea how incredibly special he was until the day of our meeting. If you'll allow me, I want..." I reach for the ring in her grasp and hold it out, ready for her finger. "...you to please agree to marry me, to let me tell you and the entire world that I love you, that you are the one woman who holds my heart in the palms of her hands, and I want nothing more than to spend the rest of my life with you and Jase."

Mandy takes a ragged breath. "The rest of your life..." she says softly.

I stand and pull her close. "I can't promise you one year or fifty. All I can promise is however long it is, I'll love you until my last breath." I lean back and tilt my head. "I love you, Mandy. What do you say?"

"I-I...Jase?"

"I want the package deal. And he already said yes."

Though her eyes are still glassy, her smile blossoms. "You asked Jase?"

"I asked your dad. Jase and I talked in less specifics. He told me that he likes it when you're happy and that when I'm with you two, you're happy."

"Jase said that?"

I nod.

"And my dad?"

"Beautiful, I've gotten yeses from everyone but you...and right now that's scaring me."

She lifts her left hand and spreads her fingers apart.

It takes me a second to remember the ring. As I approach her fourth finger with the white gold band and diamond solitaire, I ask again, "Mandy Wells, will you marry me?"

The ring fits perfectly. Sally helped me with that.

She nods. "Yes, Malcolm." She looks down at the ring and back to me. "I love you, too. I have since that first night. I was scared to admit it, even to myself." The tears are still flowing. "But now that I have, can we promise something?"

She loves me.

"Anything," I say.

"Let's not say forever. Instead, let's say we'll be together for one night...a night that goes on forever."

CHAPTER

Twenty Nine

Mandy
A year and a half later

"You know, you're insatiable," Malcolm says as I lift my very pregnant body over his and slide down on his hard rod.

"Hmmm," I hum. "I think you can blame hormones."

His deep laugh reverberates from his chest to my hands as I wiggle, getting us as close as two people can be—as close as two people can be when one is eight months pregnant and her midsection is roughly the size of a beach ball.

"I'm not complaining," he says as his blue eyes sparkle my direction.

I move slowly up and down, watching his satisfied smile. "Yeah, you don't seem to mind."

"I don't. But I miss the sailor talk."

Moving my hands to his shoulders, I continue to adjust, enjoying the friction as his thumb strokes my oversensitive clit.

"Fuck," I whisper, bending as close as I can to his ear.

"Louder, beautiful."

Holding my hips, he moves me with more force as I sit straighter. My head rolls backward and back arches. I'm not sure if it is the hormones or simply Malcolm, but as I continue to move, I'm consumed with the fullness and friction.

"I-I can't be louder," I pant more than say. "I don't want Jase to hear."

Malcolm laughs again as he palms my breast. "He can't hear. He's still asleep. If he weren't, he'd be in here." He leans upward and sucks one of my nipples and then the other. "Have I mentioned that I love how big your tits have gotten?"

"A few times," I say, enjoying the sensation of his caresses.

My knees flex. As our speed increases, I'm not the only one whispering cuss words. Malcolm too is murmuring them. There's a low roar of *fucks* as his neck strains and grip tightens. There may not be any new words in his repertoire, but I love the way the few he says rumble to my core, just like his deep voice and hard cock.

Once I collapse against the pillows, Malcolm leans my way. "Are you sure you are up for the Children's Museum today?"

I nod my head. "It's air conditioned, so yes." I reach down and stroke his dick. "You, however, are definitely more up than I am, but yes, I want to go." I stifle a yawn. "Maybe a nap first."

Malcolm kisses my forehead. "You're stunning, all sex exhausted, Mrs. P."

"Yes," I run my hand over my stretched skin. "I feel stunning."

He kisses me again. "You should. You're glowing."

"I want to go to the museum. We promised Jase, and before we know it, his little brother will be here. I don't want Jase to think we aren't spending enough time with him."

Malcolm leans down, placing his hand and lips near my huge midsection. "Did you hear that, Jack? Your mommy's afraid you'll be taking all our time."

My smile grows as Malcolm talks to our not-yet-born son. Just as with Jase, he carries on conversations, just the same as if he's talking to other adults. He never talks down as if Jase can't understand, and he asks Jase's opinion. It's fulfilling to hear and see how Jase responds. I have no doubt Jack will be the same way, enthralled by all his daddy says and does.

Even now, I fight tears as I hear Jack's name from Malcolm's lips.

That's probably hormones too.

No matter the cause of my emotion, I wasn't sure about naming our son after Jackson. It wasn't my idea, but the more

Malcolm argued his case, the more it seemed like the right thing to do.

Sometimes I feel like the cartoon Grinch as my heart grows bigger and bigger, allowing more and more room for the men I love. The fact that Malcolm isn't threatened by the part of my heart that will always belong to Jackson makes the love we share even that much more special. I'm constantly awed to wordless wonder as each day Malcolm does something else to make me, Jase, and I'm sure, soon, Jack, feel special. I never thought I'd find what we have, and I'm so thankful that Mom and Sally talked me into going out for just one night.

"What she doesn't realize..." Malcolm goes on as if Jack were listening and answering. "...is that your brother will want to spend more time with you than he will with us. We're the old people."

"Hey, speak for yourself," I say, "I'm not old." As I talk, Jack moves and one side of my tummy is suddenly higher than the other.

""That is so cool," Malcolm exclaims, his hand firmly on our son.

"Oh, he's as active as his brother."

"I think he likes it when his mommy and daddy are close."

My lips twitch. "How close?"

"Well, Mrs. P., I suppose that's up to him and up to you. I'm game for another round."

"I thought you said *I* was insatiable."

His hands roam down my body. "I'm just thinking of you. I know how much you like it...and as much as I love you riding my cock, I also love it when you're on your knees."

I shake my head. Malcolm's right. I do like...well, everything he does. And the bigger Jack gets, the more different positions we explore. As it is, round one has me worn out. Shaking my head, I curl my body as close as I can and rest my head on his chest. "Nap first, and then Children's Museum."

Malcolm laughs, making his broad chest shake. "Maybe you are old."

"Pregnant, not old." I lift my eyes until they meet the dazzling blue I adore. "And after the museum we can go to Roy's for ice cream."

"See, you are insatiable."

I lower my head again to his shoulder with a giggle. He's right again. I'm either hungry or horny. Sex and food are my two current desires. Oh, and a third—sleep. I'm also tired.

"All right..." He strokes my hair. "...beautiful, don't worry about Jase. He's excited about being a big brother. I'm sure that from the first time he and Jack meet, they'll be best buds."

I lift my face toward Malcolm and kiss his full, sexy lips. "Hmm," I hum once our kiss ends. "I'm glad we met."

"Me too. I'm glad you agreed to one night."

THE END

I hope you're smiling just as much as I was when I finished writing Mandy and Malcolm's story.
Thank you again for indulging in my lighter side!
My dark is not forgotten and I promise that I have plans. Please let me know if along with my dark, you'd like more of Leatha, the lighter side of Aleatha. And if this is your first journey into my lighter side, PLUS ONE, another stand-alone, is also available.
Thank you for reading.

WHAT TO DO NOW

LEND IT: Did you enjoy ONE NIGHT? Do you have a friend who'd enjoy ONE NIGHT? The ebook of ONE NIGHT may be lent one time. Sharing is caring!

RECOMMEND IT: Do you have multiple friends who'd enjoy ONE NIGHT? Tell them about it! Call, text, post, tweet...your recommendation is the nicest gift you can give to an author!

REVIEW IT: Tell the world. Please go to the retailer where you purchased this book, as well as Goodreads, and write a review. Please share your thoughts about ONE NIGHT on:

*Amazon, *ONE NIGHT*, Customer Reviews

*Barnes & Noble, *ONE NIGHT,* Customer Reviews

*iBooks, *ONE NIGHT*, Customer Reviews

*Goodreads.com/Aleatha Romig

If you liked this book you can find more of Aleatha's Lighter Ones here: www.aleatharomig.com/aleatha-s-lighter-ones

BOOKS BY ALEATHA ROMIG

ALEATHA'S LIGHTER ONES:

PLUS ONE

Stand-alone fun, sexy romance

Released May 2017

ONE NIGHT

Stand-alone, sexy contemporary romance

Coming September 2017

THE INFIDELITY SERIES:

BETRAYAL

Book #1

(October 2015)

CUNNING

Book #2

(January 2016)

DECEPTION

Book #3

(May 2016)

ENTRAPMENT

Book #4

(September 2016)

FIDELITY

Book #5

(January 2017)

RESPECT

A stand-alone Infidelity novel

(Coming January 2018)

THE CONSEQUENCES SERIES:

CONSEQUENCES

(Book #1)

Released August 2011

TRUTH

(Book #2)

Released October 2012

CONVICTED

(Book #3)

Released October 2013

REVEALED

(Book #4)

Previously titled: Behind His Eyes Convicted: The Missing Years

Re-released June 2014

BEYOND THE CONSEQUENCES

(Book #5)

Released January 2015Released January 2015

CONSEQUENCES COMPANION READS:

BEHIND HIS EYES-CONSEQUENCES

Released January 2014
BEHIND HIS EYES-TRUTH

Released March 2014

THE LIGHT SERIES:

Published through Thomas and Mercer Amazon exclusive
INTO THE LIGHT

Released 2016
AWAY FROM THE DARK

Released 2016

TALES FROM THE DARK SIDE SERIES:

INSIDIOUS

(All books in this series are stand-alone erotic thrillers)

Released October 2014
DUPLICITY

(Completely unrelated to book #1)

Release TBA

ABOUT THE AUTHOR

Aleatha Romig is a New York Times, Wall Street Journal, and USA Today bestselling author who lives in Indiana, USA. She grew up in Mishawaka, graduated from Indiana University, and is currently living south of Indianapolis. Aleatha has raised three children with her high school sweetheart and husband of over thirty years. Before she became a full-time author, she worked days as a dental hygienist and spent her nights writing. Now, when she's not imagining mind-blowing twists and turns, she likes to spend her time a with her family and friends. Her other pastimes include reading and creating heroes/anti-heroes who haunt your dreams!

Aleatha released her first novel, CONSEQUENCES, in August of 2011. CONSEQUENCES became a bestselling series with five novels and two companions released from 2011 through 2015. The compelling and epic story of Anthony and Claire Rawlings has graced more than half a million e-readers. Aleatha released the first of her series TALES FROM THE DARK SIDE, INSIDIOUS, in the fall of 2014. These stand alone thrillers continue Aleatha's twisted style with an increase in heat.

In the fall of 2015, Aleatha moved head first into the world of dark romantic suspense with the release of BETRAYAL, the first of her five novel INFIDELITY series that has taken the reading world by storm. She also began her traditional publishing career with Thomas and Mercer. Her books INTO THE LIGHT and

AWAY FROM THE DARK were published through this mystery/thriller publisher in 2016.

2017 brings Aleatha's first "Leatha, the lighter side of Aleatha" with PLUS ONE, a fun, sexy romantic comedy.

Aleatha is a "Published Author's Network" member of the Romance Writers of America and PEN America. She is represented by Kevan Lyon of Marsal Lyon Literary Agency.

Stay connected with Aleatha

Do you love Aleatha's writing? Do you want to keep up to date about what's coming next?

Do you like EXCLUSIVE content (never-released scenes, never-released excerpts, and more)? Would you like the monthly chance to win prizes (signed books and gift cards)? Then sign up today for Aleatha's monthly newsletter and stay informed on all things Aleatha Romig.

NEWSLETTER: Recipients of Aleatha's Newsletter receive exclusive material and offers.

Aleatha's Newsletter Sign-up

You can also find Aleatha@

Goodreads:
http://www.goodreads.com/author/show/5131072.Aleatha_Romig
Instagram: http://instagram.com/aleatharomig

You may also listen to Aleatha Romig books on Audible:

Aleatha's Audibles

aleatharomig.com
aleatharomig@gmail.com

CPSIA information can be obtained
at www.ICGtesting.com
Printed in the USA
BVOW06s0712261117
501266BV00012B/239/P